Pip hasn't worked in a decade when her new agent calls un-expectedly. A movie role is on offer, and Magda Quest Saxer wants an answer in less than a week. She gives Pip an implied ultimatum. Take it and fly to Sydney for a screen test. Turn it down it and never work again. With no one else to advise her, Pip consults the cats. Kittisack and Amberjill are probably real. Lupin's cat is made of pottery. All of them think she ought to take the role.

This disruption is bad enough, but Cousin Lupin's legacy is confusing. Pip risks a call to ask what it's all about, and within the hour she's off on a magical mystery tour on a yacht crewed by people she doesn't know.

It's bewildering stuff, especially when one of the crew goes missing and the other two don't seem to care. Pip cares, but dialling triple zero has its complications when someone nearby can make the phone jump right out of her hand.

Performing Pippin Pearmain 2
Copyright © 2022 Lark Westerly
ISBN: 978-1-4874-3706-0
Cover art by Martine Jardin

Published by eXtasy Books Inc

Look for us online at:
www.eXtasybooks.com

Performing Pippin Pearmain 2
Performing Pippin Pearmain

By

Lark Westerly

DEDICATION

For everyone who likes a bit of fun and magic in life. If magic doesn't oblige, you can always read about it and write about it too!

AUTHOR'S NOTE

Fiction and Reality

Major places, such as Tasmania, the city of Sydney and the state of Victoria certainly do exist. So does Bass Strait. The towns of Jellico Bay and Delmsford are made up, as is Delphinium Island. The disappearances in Bass Strait that Pip recalls never happened, but similar disappearances have, as they do in just about any stretch of water. There are over fifty islands in Bass Strait, between Tasmania and mainland Australia. Hypatia and Citrus Islands are *not* two of them. The Jellico diamonds Pip collects on the beach and stores in her collection of porcelain shoes are also invented. They are vaguely based on Killiecrankie diamonds, which are topaz pebbles found at Killiecrankie Bay on Flinders Island. Tektites do exist and are sometimes made into rings. Tulips come in a lot of exciting varieties, but as far as I know firebird tulips exist only in Pip's world.

Pip's story covers a year, taking her from her reclusive cottage in Jellico Bay to her old hometown of Delmsford, to the magical fossmere, on to Sydney and thence to Delphinium Island. The nine books compile into one continuing story, slowly revealing the mystery and magic that has been part of Pip's world all along.

And how did I come to write Pip's story? It all began with a flower show...and a bucket.

Book 2, the one you are about to read, begins in Lemonwood Cottage, travels to the coast and thence to the yacht, *Tulpenmanie*. Now, here's a refresher of what happened in the first part of the story.

The story so far…

Book One

Introducing Pippin Pearmain—small, eccentric, determined, sixty-six, and ruled by cats. Until a decade ago, Pip earned her living by playing offbeat roles on stage and screen, but after her mother and her agent died in the same week, the offers dried up and she moved to Jellico Bay. During a visit to her old hometown she encountered her cousins, Lupin de Leon and Juniper "Jan" Sharman. They, and Jan's daughter, Clarkia, were the only remaining members of the Laurel-Pearmain-de-Leon family. Over afternoon tea at the Delmsford Flower Show, Pip revealed her long-held secret: her bucket list, a literal list of interesting buckets. In return, her cousins wrote down their secrets.

Home in her cottage with the original cat and the back-up cat, which communicate with her in what she thinks of as Cat-Morse, Pip read the secrets. Jan identified herself as the novelist Juniper Gin. Lupin's secret was shocking—she had just a few months to live.

After Lupin's passing, Jan met the cats Kittisack and Amberjill and received a bucket Pip had promised her for Lupin's last repose. They discussed the provenance of a family heirloom—two copies of a book called *Grandmother's Sunshine*. Lacking heirs, Pip had once offered her copy to a young friend, whose mother refused to let her accept it. A call from Jan's daughter prompted Jan to dash off, leaving Pip with Lupin's legacy—an envelope and a pottery cat.

PART ONE. INVISIBLE INK: APRIL 2022

CHAPTER ONE. DRAMA QUEEN

Cousin Jan had gone off in a hurry to meet her daughter, who bore the unlikely name of Clarkia.

That left Pippin Pearmain alone in Lemonwood Cottage — unless one counted the cats who were her housemates.

The original cat, who looked like a seal point Siamese tom, and who answered — sometimes — to the name of Kittisack, had been around for the whole ten years of Pip's tenure in Jellico Bay. His apprentice, the back-up cat, whose name was probably Amberjill, was of much more recent vintage. The third cat, newly arrived and even more newly unswaddled from its cocoon of tissue paper and sticky tape, had been made of pottery by Jan's recently deceased sister, Lupin. Therefore, it would be forever known as Lupin's cat.

Jan said the thing gave her the willies. Kittisack and Amberjill seemed inclined to worship it. They suggested it had been blessed by a guardian. Pip didn't know what they meant by that. She didn't really feel like asking.

Nevertheless, she was glad to have Lupin's cat at the cottage. It was so bizarre, so ugly in form and yet so lovely in colour and decoration, that Pip would never grow bored with the contrast.

Besides, there was every indication that Lupin herself, tastefully stored in a handsome old bucket, would be spending six months of the year on the mantel along with the cat...*just like Persephone after she ate the half-dozen pomegranate seeds*, as Lupin had put it in the farewell letter she'd written to Pip.

1

Pip didn't know if this would really happen. It was one of several matters she hadn't yet discussed with Jan. They might have got around to it if Jan's daughter Clarkia hadn't texted a message which sent Jan off in a hurry.

So much for wondering what I'd do with Jan for a full day…

What will happen will happen, I suppose… That's what Little Nanna Pearmain used to say.

Pip shrugged and picked up the patisserie box from the table. The cats had raided it while she farewelled Jan. She shook the crumbs they'd left onto a folded newspaper. Maybe Bill the blue-tongued lizard would like them. If not, then the ants probably would, and Bill might like *them*. Maybe. She knew he liked hardboiled egg and tomatoes, so why not ants? Pip took the crumbs to the woodpile where Bill mostly lived, returned to the kitchen, and shifted her attention to Lupin's cat.

The larcenous cats had been giving it some love after they finished with the tarts, so she cleaned cat slobber off it with one of the wet-wipes her cousin had left on the table. She carried it to the mantelpiece and set it carefully between Little Pop Pearmain's brass candlesticks. He'd made them from discarded shell casings after the war.

"Let me know if you'd rather be somewhere else," she said to Lupin's cat.

The figurine said nothing, but Pip was aware of its magnetic pull. What had the cats Cat-Morsed? It was charmed by a guardian . . .and was also unbreakable.

It was somewhat and oddly familiar. She had no idea why. It was one-of-a-kind, and no one would have wanted it or even been able to have copied it.

That's just creepy.

She turned her back. She would *not* start worshipping a pottery cat. It was too much like the golden calf of the Israelites.

Why a calf, anyway? Didn't the Hebrews have enough gold to make a whole cow?

She glanced over to the corner where the Clancy bucket had been. She'd miss that reminder of her old friend Mister Clancy, but it was fitting that Jan should take it for storing Lupin's ashes. It was a contribution.

Absently, she employed the used wet-wipe to collect the remaining tart crumbs from her table.

She was giving the wooden tabletop a final wipe-over with a dry cloth when she spotted the scattered papers on the floor.

Those cats again…

It wasn't like them to be so clumsy, or so destructive.

Some of the paper was the tissue-and-tape shell that had encased Lupin's cat. It was clawed to tatters, no doubt by the diligent cats. Maybe it was some kind of ritual. Possibly they were making sure no one ever used it to re-swaddle Lupin's cat or, possibly, them. Who knew why cats did what they did?

Pip put the tatters in the bin.

Another paper was the envelope Jan had given her, miraculously unmolested. It had bank account details in it, she recalled — another legacy from Lupin.

Jan had headed her off at the pass when she suggested it should go to Lupin's more natural heirs…her sister and niece. It was for Pip or for no one.

Trust Lupin to be dictatorial, even beyond the grave.

Oh. Lupin hasn't got a grave. She has a bucket instead.

The thought was warming. Graves often seemed so cold, and so remote from everyday concerns. A bucket was pleasantly domestic, and the Clancy bucket was undeniably fine.

Pip put the envelope on the mantelpiece next to Lupin's cat and bent to retrieve the third item of the under-table scatter. It was another envelope — one Jan hadn't mentioned. Maybe she would have if Clarkia hadn't called.

Pip hoped it wasn't something Jan should have taken with her.

I could text her…or ring her. She might have her phone patched through to hands-free. She can't have got far.

3

She turned the envelope over and saw her name written on the front in Lupin's characteristic elegant script, so different from Jan's left-handed slant and her own meticulously tiny green lettering.

Pippin Picotee Pearmain.

The envelope was lightly sealed, but not as if Lupin had meant it. More as if it had succumbed to pressure when Jan stuffed it in her grey case, Pip decided.

Why the grey case, anyway? Why not stuff Lupin's cat and two envelopes in her lavender bag? Maybe the case was Lupin's.

That seemed likely.

She put the envelope on the table.

I ought to fix my bucket list. I don't have the Clancy bucket anymore. I need to add the information that it's going home with Jan.

Maybe I need another cuppa…I wonder if Bill will like those crumbs. Do blue-tongues eat pastry? The birds might if the ants don't. The magpies…no, they'll want cheese, as usual. Better get them some, because otherwise they'll be warbling accusations through the window.

A strange buzz made her glance behind her, in case Lupin's cat had decided to make a weird crooning noise.

Idiot. You're humming again.

Odd that she should notice. Her high-pitched habitual hum had always annoyed Lupin.

I need to —

Pip looked around for inspiration.

You need to open that letter, Kittisack signalled from where he lurked by her feet. He must have come into the kitchen while she vacillated.

"No. I don't want to."

Do it.

"No."

His claws came out to pluck at her ankle.

"*No!*" Pip said forcefully.

The original cat withdrew his paw. *Why not?*

"Because I don't take orders from a larcenous cat."

The tarts were abandoned. It was right for us to eat them.

"They were on the table! Since when does that constitute tart-abandonment?"

You left them. Anything might have got to them.

"Anything did. Two anythings. Two cats, to be precise."

All this to avoid opening an envelope.

Pip sighed in exasperation. "Oh, all right. If you *must* have it, I don't want to open it because last time I read something Lupin wrote, it told me she was dying. I got reshuffled to the top of the family pack. I—" She clutched at her chest. "Kittisack, am I having a panic attack? I don't feel quite myself."

Nonsense. You're being a drama queen. Listen.

"Tell no one?" That was the original cat's usual mantra.

Who are you going to tell? Pippin Picotee Pearmain, whatever is in this letter can't hurt you, or anyone else. Your cousin Lupin has gone to glory.

That was such an odd thing for a cat to communicate, but Pip decided she liked it better than *died* or the mealy-mouthed *passed away*. She tried to remember where she had heard or read the term before.

Ah! It was in a story from *Grandmother's Sunshine*. The story called *The Lovely Land*.

You never know. It might be good news in the envelope, Kittisack persuaded.

Pip sought for any way it could possibly be good news.

Unless...could Lupin be revealing news of a secret baby? Lupin had been away at university when Pip was fifteen. She'd come back for holidays and weekends but, as Jan had said of her own seldom-seen daughter, a baby *could* be fitted into the gaps between family reunions. Maybe Lupin *had* done her duty to the family bloodline. Pip never had.

I might have a niece to carry on the Laurel blood. No, it can't be a niece, because I never had a sister or a brother. It would be a cousin. Once removed.

She recalled with shame that she already had one of those. Jan's daughter Clarkia had been around for decades.

I should have tried to know her. She's lost her only aunt — or does she have other aunts on her father's side?

She ought to have known the answer to that. Jan had been married to Mark Sharman for years — but Pip wasn't sure if she'd know him if he sauntered through her door without warning. She hadn't even gone to the wedding...

Why not? I'm sure Jan would have invited me. Oh... that's right... we were shooting Ruby Shoes Emporium. *I was dancing as The Dorothy while Jan was saying I do.*

Jan understood why I wasn't there. She knew I had to work.

Her husband's family — didn't. They thought I should have turned down the part or asked for time off. They have no idea how these things work. But — fair enough. I probably wouldn't know how their jobs work either.

I should get to know Clarkia now. She's the only relative I have, other than Jan...unless...

No. If Lupin had a baby, she'd have kept it and brought it up with proper pronouns and an appreciation of cherry-titted nibbles. She wouldn't have kept it a secret.

Cherry-titted nibbles. That reminded her — again — of the *LL Gina Delmsford Hawkins Kitchen Manual* where the recipe for those confections — which were properly called cherry jam drops — might be found.

I'll just go and find my copy of the book — in case I want to make some. I'm sure I have some of the cherry jam I made last summer. Might have to get some more butter, though. I'll check. Then I can go to the shops and get some.

Open that envelope, the original cat signalled in relentless Cat-Morse.

He flexed his claws in a meaningful way and warbled a loud challenge in his croaky Siamese voice.

Pip jumped and gasped.

Cat-Morse was a silent language. Hearing a vocalisation

gave her the creeps.

She picked up the envelope and stuck her thumb in the flap.

Her phone rang.

Pip dropped the envelope on the table. Maybe Jan had missed her wet-wipes already.

"Hello?" she said breathlessly.

"Are I speaking with Pippin Pearmain?"

"Yes."

It wasn't Jan.

CHAPTER TWO. AGENT

"You're a difficult woman to track down, Pippin Pearmain," the voice on the other end of the call said.

"Do I know you?" Pip asked.

There was a pause. Then the voice said, "No you don't, but—"

"Goodbye then." Pip hovered her thumb over the end-call button.

The voice chuckled. "My word, you're perfect."

Tiny Pippin Pearmain is perfect in the role of the ephemeral Dream Child…as the enigmatic doppelganger…as the unseen leprechaun…as the Old Child in The Many Selves of Merry…*as The Dorothy.*

Pip waited a split second too long, which gave the voice a chance to speak again.

"You don't know me, Miss Pearmain but I'm your agent by default."

"You *what*?" Pip started to hum.

The voice, gruff but female, chuckled again. "I *do* have the correct Pippin Pearmain, I trust? Pippin Picotee Pearmain?"

Pip stayed silent.

"You were signed with the Sullivan Gilbert Agency in nineteen sixty-two—is that correct?"

"Yes, and I still am, as far as I know. They pay me residuals."

Pip supposed they still did. Sully had set it up that way, and no one had yet complained that her bill payments were not executing. The payments happened automatically. Sully had set those up as well, and when her old bank was absorbed by a more aggressive one, Pip paid the new manager a visit and informed him that he, or a reliable member of staff, was going to ensure that her arrangement with his predecessor continued.

"We don't offer that service, Ms Pearmain," the bank manager had explained in a bored and superior tone. His gaze had strayed to his mobile phone.

"Miss. The letter you sent to me assured me I could enjoy all the benefits of my original bank, the one I have used all my life, and which *you* bought without reference to what I and the other customers wanted."

The bank manager had produced a sound halfway between a scoff and an indulgent chuckle. "I think you'll find your old bank didn't offer that service, either…not in the last two decades, anyway."

And two decades ago you were down by the bridge fishing for tiddleys.

"They did to me. I had it set up in perpetuity."

"My dear Ms Pearmain—"

"Miss."

"I beg your pardon?"

"Miss. I am not miserable, married or a manuscript."

"Miss Pearmain."

"Would you like me to tell you the dictionary definition of *perpetuity?*"

"Whatever arrangement you made with your former bank—"

"My former bank is part of this bank because you absorbed it. The letter you sent me assured me I could enjoy all the benefits of my original bank, the one I have used all my life, and which *you* bought without reference to what I and the other customers wanted."

He looked harassed.

"All the benefits. I am assured of *all* the benefits. That bill-

9

payment in perpetuity is a benefit. I enjoy it. I will continue to enjoy it."

"I suppose we could set up—"

"It's set up already. That's what *in perpetuity* means. You don't set up the sunrise, right? It happens. It was set up in perpetuity."

"There may be a better product for your needs."

"This one works perfectly for my needs. Do not try to reinvent the wheel. Oh, and while you're at it, you can ensure that my active accrual account continues to accrue."

"As explained in our letter, we no longer offer that product. In its place, we have a superior product called the special saver. The annual fee is waived when you spend a thousand—"

"I don't *spend* from the active accrual account. It compounds interest. There are no fees. There never have been."

"That product is not in line with—"

"All the benefits, you promised. In writing. I have the letter here."

Pip remembered the annoyance on the young manager's face. She supposed she had been a wee bit hard on him but then…

People shouldn't make promises they have no intention of keeping. Neither should they lie to customers by pretending the new account that pays much less interest is a better product. Better for whom? Better for the bank, that's who.

"Residuals," she repeated into the phone.

"Hm?" the voice on the phone said, in the tone of someone who is a bit lost in an off-track conversation.

Pip hummed while she waited for the person to find herself, thinking of all the things Sully had done to make her life easier.

Sully had died back in 2012, just three days after Little Mum and the last cat, Duster, who had sauntered off together, just as they had sauntered around the garden in life.

Sully had been nursing her favourite sludge-black coffee on Little Mum's rose brocade rocker, telling a scurrilous story about an unnamed celebrity.

Pip, half-listening in her grief, had heard Sully pause for effect before she delivered the punchline...

That punchline never came.

Sully had gone beyond with barely a grimace, leaving behind a Rohrbach splodge of coffee that stained Little Mum's brocade and a scurrilous tale forever without a pay-off.

Little Mum's death had been Too Much for Pip. Duster's death had been another crack in her veneer.

Sully's sudden passing had splintered the façade wide open.

Sullivan Gilbert had always had Pip's best interests in mind, because, as she said frankly, if Pip earned, so did her agency, and a happy and productive performer made for a happily solvent agent.

"I doubt if anyone is paying you residuals, since the company went tits up back in twenty-nineteen," the voice on the phone informed her.

Pip jerked herself away from the memory of vanquished bank managers and the vision of spoiled brocade. She wished — now — that she'd tried to match the rose brocade and had the chair re-covered. "Are you sure? Nobody told *me*."

"I'm not surprised. Hard woman to find, as I said. When Sullivan Gilbert went into receivership, I bought up the remaining contracts. Most of the assets had retired or moved on years before — jumping ship when the principal of the agency died. You, on the other hand, were a puzzle. No one had viable contact details for you, but you had never officially retired. You weren't listed on anyone else's books. None of the studios I checked with had a clue where you were."

"What *is* all this about?" Pip reflected they couldn't have tried so very hard to contact her. She'd had the same phone number for years — since well before Sully died. Besides, just how many Pippin Pearmains could there be in a state the size of Tasmania? Or should that be Pippins Pearmain for a perfect plural…

She'd flitted from Delmsford in 2012, but she'd moved no more than two and a half hours from her original home. Anyone with half an hour to spare could have found her if they'd given it an honest try. This person was proof of that.

"Are you firing me?" she enquired. She'd never been sure exactly who could fire whom in her situation, and she wasn't having any truck with euphemisms such as *letting her go.* She and Sully would *never* have fired one another.

"Hard to fire a person who hasn't had a paying gig in over a decade. Practically superfluous, one might say."

Pip jerked the phone away from her ear and glowered at it. She said, "I *am* well over sixty."

The voice scoffed, distantly. "You're a spring lamb frisking through the daisies, compared with some. Now that I have your attention…I called because I have a possible part for you."

CHAPTER THREE. PERDITA

Pip brought the phone back to her ear.

"Really?"

"I'm not in the habit of leading folk up the garden path. I wouldn't have gone to the trouble of tracking you down you just to tell you porky pies."

"Some people do. They're usually trying to scam me or else they want to sell me something, or occasionally tell me why I can't have what I *can* have." Pip had no idea how she felt about the prospect of working again. She said, cautiously, "Who are you again?"

"I'm the person who rescued the Sullivan Gilbert Agency from the doldrums. Magda Quest Saxer from Magdala Gallery."

"Oh." Pip had heard of Magda Quest Saxer, but surely she ought to be dead? Didn't she represent visual artists way back in the 1950s?

Almost before my time.

The woman said, "*Oh* is a ringing endorsement, Miss Pearmain. If it's any comfort to you, I knew Sully well, back in the day. She was younger than me, but we were drinking friends. I'm a Tom Cat Hill whiskey woman from way back, but Sully was all about the beer. She used to bitch at the relative costs when it was her round. Mind, she did drink Fagus Ale, which was a wee bit pricier than your general malt-and-hops slosh. For all her bitching, I was sorry to hear she'd gone to glory. She was my oldest friend except for Peter P…and he gets his knickers in a knot when I reach for the whiskey. Always did."

13

Pip nearly dropped the phone. *Gone to glory.* That was the second time she'd heard that quaintly old-fashioned term in less than an hour. The first time had been from Kittisack, who surely shouldn't have known it.

"Are you still there, Miss Pearmain?"

Pip admitted that she was.

"I didn't make a move on the agency then because it was none of my business and I had plenty on my plate anyway. When I heard the people who took over from Sully were running it straight into the ground—I stepped in." She snorted. "No one was pleased with me. I wasn't pleased with them. I rescued the agency with a bit of help from an embryo finance wizard called Henry Dark. Know him?"

"No."

"He was a downy little junior nerd, but he knew his stuff, even then. He still hangs on the fringes of the performing world—his wife is the roadie for an indie band.

"So, do you want to hear more on this potential part, or not?"

"Okay." Pip couldn't imagine what part she could be up for over a decade after her last role. She added, "You do know I'm not exactly a mainstream actor, right? I never went to stage school. I don't do Lady Macbeth or romantic leads or ditzy mums in sit-coms—never did."

"I've got your resume in front of me. It's out of date, but I've seen you in a good many of your roles. Child star in the sixties, ingenue in the seventies…and you just went on from there. My daughter's a fan. She has said more than once that Pippin Pearmain cannot be classified because she's unclassifiable."

"Is that a good thing?"

"In general, no. Most folk prefer the classifiable. It's tidier."

Pip heard the rustle of paper.

"Right. This new film is an arty-farty piece with the

working title *Half-Life of the Lost*. The protagonist is a coma-tose woman — no, don't interrupt. That's not the role you're up for. You'd be wasted.

"This character, Perdita, went into a coma on her wedding day, for reasons unspecified. She's been asleep for sixty years."

"Is that possible?" Pip interrupted. She knew a lot about the first Queen Elizabeth, spiteful lemon trees, buckets, and Cat-Morse, but she wasn't well up on the facts of comas.

"Who knows? A case of thirty-seven years has been documented, and I believe there was also one of forty-two."

"Did they ever wake up?"

"In a word — no."

"What's the longest coma someone has woken up from?"

"Twenty-something years — Miss Pearmain, I am not an encyclopaedia. Do you want to know about this part, or not?"

"Okay," Pip said. After all, she wasn't going to be the comatose protagonist.

"Perdita ages slowly, and visibly, throughout the film. So do the people who visit her. We see them in different clothing, with different hairstyles, but we only ever see them in the room with Perdita. Sometimes they come alone, and sometimes they visit together and hold conversations, or discuss her situation. Over the years some stop coming, and others use her as a confessional. A child who has never known her comes on her first day of school, her wedding day, and on her own sixtieth birthday. Someone goes into cardiac arrest during a visit, and everyone assumes the code blue was for Perdita — you get the picture."

Pip saw it could be a pretentious mess, or a poignant commentary on family and the human condition. "Where would I come in, if not as Perdita?"

Magda Saxer didn't say *gotcha* audibly, but Pip felt it hovering in the ether.

"The brief is for a performer who can represent the consciousness of the main character. She can move freely around the room where Perdita sleeps, and she's ageless. She breaks the fourth wall from time to time, and she occasionally speaks to the characters, or comments on them, but none of them knows she's there. She's a voice for the voiceless...sharp, witty, and yet curiously naïve as she has no existence outside the room. She moves like a somnambulist, or strides around, or dances, according to mood. She changes her clothing to fit the seasons and the changing times, just as Perdita would have done. At one point, she scares away someone who would have done Perdita harm."

Pip discovered she was nodding, which was ridiculous, because the agent couldn't see her. "I could do that," she said.

"Grand!"

"It's the same role I've always played."

"Oh?"

Pip ran over the characters she recalled — the tree nymph, Arabella Junket, Dream Child, Sleepwalker, the doppelganger, The Dorothy, Marigold Heriot, Teacup Beloved, Merry, Swan and all the others. They were all observers, peripheral or catalysts, oblique and not necessarily there. Only Marigold Heriot from *House of Heriot* and Tanner from *Dingo Nights* had been somewhat different...

"I know exactly how to play it," she said. She extended one arm and danced a few steps, swaying and passing her hand in front of a clueless observer.

"You'll be booked to fly out for a screen test in ten days' time."

"What?" Pip paused on tiptoe.

"Screen test. In Sydney. It's being filmed on the sound stage at Delphinium Island — filmed as a play, using a single set with variable lighting and a soundscape of fiddle and flute. Arty-farty, as I said."

Pip went cold as she lowered her heels to the floor.

"Are you there, Miss Pearmain?"

"May I have time to consider it?"

Magda Saxer sighed. "I can give you seven days, tops. After that the offer goes away, and I call the next name on my list who will be understandably affronted to be called so late in the day."

"Who is that?" Pip was buying time, but she was also genuinely curious. She had wondered occasionally what actor or actors had stepped in to fill the vacuum left by Tiny Pippin Pearmain.

"I won't tell you."

"Sully would have."

"I'm not Sully. Sully cosseted you. She treated you as a child. Fair enough when you *were* one. I won't do that. I'll ring you at eight a.m. today week. If you don't answer—"

"You'll call back."

"I'll call the next name on my list, and you won't be hearing from me again."

The phone was on dead air.

Pip took it away from her ear and stared at it in outrage.

Eight in the morning today week was *not* seven days. It was six days and a few hours. It was also the time of her daily date with lemon juice and water, after her ballet practice.

Her sense of grievance grew.

The woman had made an unreasonable offer and hung up on her.

No one hung up on Pippin Pearmain...if she didn't count the creeps who wanted to scam her or sell her funeral insurance.

And Jan. She hung up on me...

She looked down into four wide unblinking eyes—two blue and two of autumn gold.

The cats must have listened in.

All the cats.

Pip tilted her gaze to Lupin's cat, whose green eyes squinted in different directions but who had undoubtedly listened in too.

CHAPTER FOUR. ADVICE FROM LUPIN'S CAT

"What do you advise me to do?" Pip asked Lupin's cat. "I'm old enough to retire, and I thought I had. I still can if I want."

She thought again of Sully, who had managed her, interceded for her, and negotiated for her and in whom Little Mum Rosie and Little Dad Jon had placed such trust.

Their trust had been justified. There were no other actors or performers in the family, but Sully had advised them on setting up safe investments for the then seven-year-old Pip after her unexpected success as a tree nymph looking down on a cast of cavorting Greeks.

The play had run and run...and Pip's reviews had been universally adoring.

Sully had told Pip's parents, and Pip, quite frankly that most child performers had a built-in use-by date.

The work might stop coming at any time. There's a danger spot at puberty and another in the late teens. Any period of rapid development and change will be a problem on film because of continuity issues. If and when that happens it will be no reflection on you, or your worth, or your talent, but simply a shift in the industry requirements. You will absolutely be the same person you've always been. Do you understand, young Pippin?

Pip remembered staring, fascinated, into Sully's face with its energetic eyebrows.

Little Dad Jon had touched her shoulder. "Pippi, Miss Gilbert wants to know if you understand what she's saying. The work you do might stop suddenly and it won't be your fault."

Pip had nodded seriously. "I understand that. Can *I* stop if I want?"

Little Mum had rushed in with reassurance, but she'd stopped when Sully's eyebrows went up.

Sully had said, "You can't stop in the middle of a job. You'll have a contract, and that's like a promise you shouldn't break. *But* you can always say, *No more after the jobs we're signed for* or you might say, *I want to take a year or two years off.* Mind, if you take too much time off, there might be no jobs for you later. The studios will have found a new darling to hire. That's a risk to consider, but you need to do what's right for *you.*"

Pip had hummed her mosquito whine as she considered.

Sully had been saying something over her head to her parents. It was something like *I never have and never will knowingly make a child's life the worse for my involvement in it.*

The conversation had gone on while Pip hummed before Sully's eyebrows had been back in agile view.

"Well, Miss Pippin Pearmain? Is it a deal? You will never think it's *your* fault if the acting stops? And you will work hard at anything once you've decided it's a *yes*?"

Pip clearly remembered taking Sully's hand with its chunk of tektite set in a silver ring. They'd shaken on the deal.

Sully had given her that ring as a symbol of their bargain, and she'd kept it ever since. It was her *heaven and earth* ring, and it lived in a soft little pouch in her messenger bag where she kept important secrets.

Pip sometimes wondered, half smiling, just how many tektite-and-silver rings Sullivan Gilbert had. Did she give one to every performer she represented?

She'd never asked, in case hers wasn't as special as Sully implied.

And she *did* believe it was special—to this day. It was far more special than the seed pearl bracelets and the plush cats with the diamanté collars the studios kept giving her. Only two other gifts had come near... She used one of them from time to time, but she didn't think of the other one too often. She hadn't looked at it in years. She certainly didn't wear it.

With the promise made and the deal done, Sully had continued talking to Pippin *and* to her parents. "A few, a *very* few child performers continue to work well into adulthood. These are the exception, though, to be accepted but never expected."

"We understand that," Little Mum had agreed. "If Pip is one of the majority it will still be a useful experience for her."

"It will give her a nest-egg." Little Dad Jon had sounded approving.

"Useful for when she marries," Little Nanna Pearmain had opined.

"Or if she doesn't," Little Nanna Laurel had added.

Big Nanna de Leon had thought it was funny. "Wee Pippin the movie star!" But she'd patted Pippin gently on the shoulder. "Fancy seeing our Pippin in the films!"

"We'll be proud of you whatever you choose to do," Little Mum had said.

Despite the doubts and the careful explanations, Tiny Pippin Pearmain had proved herself one of those exceptions. She remained small and possessed an oddly ageless fey charm that was as potent at eighteen and thirty-five as it had been at seven.

Only as Sully aged and lost some of her drive and sharp business acumen did the parts, once regular and numerous, subside to a dribble then dry up altogether. The last one had been a role in an odd little film called *The Girl in the Frame* that wrapped six months before Sully herself did.

Pip had never seen that film and she'd not met any of the stars. Her part had been filmed in an art gallery over several weeks as she'd mingled and blended with an unsuspecting public in a variety of costumes and personae.

She'd been a living installation.

She remembered the person who'd set that up… His name was Wayne Ellington, and she hadn't liked him much. Neither had Sully, but as Sully liked to say, *A role is a role is a role… Do well in an uncongenial job and casting folk will remember you when a better one comes up.*

Only no other role had come up.

And this Magda Quest Saxer was *how* old? She'd said she was older than Sully, who had made it to a respectable eighty-seven when she'd died…no, *gone to glory*, back in 2012.

That couldn't possibly be right…

"So — what do I do?" Pip asked of Lupin's cat. "The woman was impertinent, and she tried to *blackmail* me."

Open that envelope.

She was unsurprised to note that Lupin's cat was every bit as skilled in Cat-Morse as Kittisack and Amberjill, and just as good at delivering a non sequitur.

How did I know you'd say something like that?

Because it's the next logical step, Kittisack signalled.

"I meant, what do I do regarding the part?"

Take it, obviously.

"You do understand I'd have to go to Sydney, then to Delphinium Island — wherever that is."

We understand. And you know where it is. It was on the television. It's a private island south of Sydney, home of Delphinium House and Arts in Tune.

Pip played what she considered was a trump card.

"If I got the part I might be away for at least two weeks, depending on the shoot. If it's as arty as Saxer said, the lighting could be fiddled with every few minutes. Who would look after you three while I'm gone?" *Not to speak of who would feed the cheese-loving magpies, visit Bill the blue-tongue and do battle with the sentient lemon.*

The cats conferred. Pip knew what they were doing, although she wasn't privy to their conversation.

She knew Lupin's cat was part of the confabulation.

That's just creepy.

The answer came from Amberjill, couched in her gentle Cat-Morse.

Clarkia will come to be with us when you make the film.

What? Why? She won't want to cat-sit. I don't know her. She doesn't know me. Why would she want to do me a favour...I'm not even an aunt, just a kind of removed cousin.

Pip left her objections unspoken, but the cat signalled, bracingly, *Juniper will be here too sometimes, settling her soul.*

It seemed the cats thought Clarkia and Jan might spend time at Lemonwood Cottage.

She remembered they'd approved of Jan.

"Would they really want to come?" she asked Lupin's cat, who was the only one who might be in a position to know.

Why would they?

It didn't answer.

"I'll open the envelope, then maybe decide," Pip said.

Do that.

Lupin's cat sounded encouraging.

CHAPTER FIVE. SLOW REVEAL BY LEMON JUICE

Pip picked up the envelope she'd dropped when the phone rang.

She'd already loosened the seal, so it opened easily.

"If this can be construed as *good* news, I'll answer my phone on Monday and go to Sydney," Pip promised the cats and the universe.

She slid the contents out.

It wasn't a letter from Lupin, as she'd feared. Apparently the writing she'd done on Pip's bucket list at the Delmsford Flower Show back in February was all the farewell her cousin had cared to give.

No acerbic words from beyond the crematorium.

Pip thought of Lupin, who had now passed into glory.

She hoped the *Final Gift* folk had sent her gently into the last goodnight. Lupin deserved their care. She'd trusted Pip to provide her with a magnificent bucket for her eternal bodily home. That was so much nicer than a grave. Every time Pip considered it, she quite fancied a bucket for herself.

I'll keep an eye out for a good one.

The envelope didn't yield a safety deposit key, or the number of a left-luggage locker somewhere in France. It wasn't the keepsake gold bar brooch Lupin had worn for years, and it certainly wasn't a birth or adoption certificate or even a baby's wrist band proclaiming *Baby de Leon — the lost heir with strawberry mark...and our family DNA.*

It was a piece of stiff white card, folded once. On the front was the blue monogram V-S perched on top of an emphatically yellow lemon. The back was blank, without even a batch number, copyright, or contact.

Pip opened it, half-expecting a snapshot of Lupin, a clipping of a death announcement or for some reason, a funeral notice.

That was daft. Lupin couldn't have sent a clipping, and she already knew from Jan *and* from Lupin that there was to be no funeral.

The inside of the card was printed in blue ink with the words —

V-S voucher
Purchaser
Recipient
Type
Date of Issue
Expiry

Each line had a space for written input, but the spaces were blank.

"What?" Pip glanced at the cats for help, but while she'd been focused on the envelope Kittisack and Amberjill had left the building. Only Lupin's cat remained, staring his mismatched challenge from intense green eyes.

Pip ran her fingers over the print. It didn't smudge. The card stock wasn't quite smooth, but that was typical of recycled or handmade paper.

A faint sound on the porch drew Pip's attention.

Must be Amberjill. The back-up cat often skittered across the grooved boards, pursuing a leaf or a feather.

This time, it seemed she had found something more solid to chase.

Holding the odd card in one hand, Pip went to see, just in case Amberjill had interfered with Bill blue-tongue. The thought gave her a *frisson* of dread. She was fond of Bill, in a casual way, and she didn't want him to be murdered.

Yet, would Amberjill see it as murder? Cats were natural predators. Amberjill would probably view Bill in the same way as Pip viewed Strawberry Heart tarts with cream.

A holiday in a bowl.

That reminded her of the crumbs in the kitchen.

Those cats ate my lush special-order tarts while I was seeing Jan off.

She tried to feel indignant.

Ask the back-up cat how she views Bill blue-tongue.

I can't. She might view me the same way — not as prey but as a somehow lesser being to be toyed with at leisure.

She's very sweet to you.

Softening me up, no doubt.

She opened the door and leaned out. The back-up cat frisked across the porch, batting her prey with alternate paws.

Pip relaxed.

"Watch out my lovely," she called. "That thing will savage you if it can."

Amberjill gave a final airy leap, using both paws to scoop and toss her dangerous plaything.

It landed on the porch swing and the back-up cat stared comically from side to side as if wondering where it had vanished.

"I'll take that." Pip picked up the lemon. It was bleeding juice from several punctures, but she wasn't overly sympathetic. In the decade or so she'd lived at Lemonwood Cottage she'd suffered more than enough slings and arrows of juice to the eye…and to any small and unprotected cut or graze . . .before she settled on the combined defences of onion goggles and industrial-strength rubber gloves.

The aroma that rose from the lacerated fruit was delightful, but Pip wasn't going to be caught out that way.

"I already drank one of your brethren this morning. I sucked it dry," she boasted.

She decided to bin the lemon and carried it into the kitchen where she briskly stripped off the peel for drying and disposed of the pith and bruised fruit in her dedicated compostscraps bucket—which was, incidentally, Number 76 on her bucket list and painted with pink roses.

She returned her attention to the card she still held in one hand.

The lemon had got its revenge with a juiced-up patch in the middle of the fold.

She froze.

Two letters stood out faintly brown where previously there had been none.

Pi.

Pi? As in Pi-R-squared?

She remembered joking about that with Lupin in familyspeak...just a few weeks ago at the flower show. Now Lupin was gone, cutting one more family-speak link. That left just the one tenuous connection with Jan and Clarkia. She had no idea if Clarkia knew the family-speak. She was of another generation.

She focused on the card.

Not Pi as in Pi-R-squared. It's the beginning of Pippin.

"Of course. It's invisible ink," she said aloud.

She thought back sixty years to when she and Lupin—Juniper had been too little—had played with invisible ink. Little Nanna Laurel had shown them how, and they'd patiently held the paper up to a candle until each message decoded.

This card hadn't been heated, but sometimes the lemon juice ink did leave a faint mark.

She shook her head in confusion, hoping juice from the savage lemon hadn't ruined the surprise by adulterating the message.

She put the card aside and washed and dried her hands.

Citric acid begone!

Then she lit a candle.

She couldn't recall how long it had used to take to reveal a message and anyway, she had no idea why Lupin had chosen to communicate this way. It was quirky, quaint and childlike, and Lupin had been none of those things.

Maybe she thought I was all of those things.

She pondered this while the card warmed, and the message swam into view.

V-S voucher

Purchaser — Lupin de Leon

Recipient — Pippin Pearmain

Type — Experience

Date of Issue — February 19th, 2022

Expiry — Ten weeks from date of issue

Contact TripV-S@V-S.com or telephone 0417TRIPVS

Pip hummed with annoyance.

She'd had enough startling phone calls lately.

She supposed she could send an email, but then — she looked at the date of issue and realised the expiry date was uncomfortably close.

She located her Mark One Pink Princess phone and keyed in the number.

CHAPTER SIX. TRIP

"V-S Office. Trip speaking."

The voice was a man's — curt and yet full of energy.

"This is Pippin Pearmain."

"Ah."

"You sound as if you've heard of me."

"I have. I have seen some of your work, and you're also the beneficiary of one of our recent vouchers."

Pip heard something rustle, and she pictured a hand turning the pages of an old ledger.

Imagination. It's all computerised these days.

"I have the entry here," the man continued. "The purchaser was Lupin de Leon."

Pip was nonplussed by the simplicity of the phone call. After the cloak and dagger of the slow reveal by lemon juice, she'd expected more mystery and less cooperation.

She waited, but the man said no more.

Unlike Magda Saxer, he did not enquire if she was still there.

Finally she said, "Tell me what all this means."

"Miss de Leon bought a voucher from us in your name."

"I understand that, but who is *us*? The card says V-S. That could mean anything."

"I was using the term loosely to cover those who work in the company. I am a largely silent partner, but sometimes I take a more active role."

Pip perceived that the ease of gaining information had been an illusion.

"What is *the company*? The card I have says V-S, but as I said, I have no clue what that stands for."

"Generally, the donor of the voucher explains things to the recipient. Since that's not possible in your case, I'll give you the five-cent tour.

"V-S stands for Vouch-Safe. That is a parent company with subsidiaries, some wholly owned and others of which we are minority shareholders. We employ a diverse range of providers, most of whom hold shares in the company, although some work only occasionally as and when..."

Pip's eyes felt as if they were glazing over. She was familiar with the condition of eye-glaze. It generally came on when someone tried to make her pay attention to something she didn't like and in which she had no interest. It was typically accompanied by humming—not the happy, busy hum of a mind in pleasurable thought, but a cold, resentful dentists' drill of a sound.

She interrupted his spiel. "You sound like a stockbroker. I don't want to know your company structure. I want to know about this voucher."

Silence.

"Mister—" She'd forgotten his name, but her gaze dropped to the contact details as revealed by the candle. "Mister Trip?"

"I was trying to formulate an answer to fit your requirements. I doubt it's possible. Bear with me."

Pip began to hum her high and drilling whine.

"Miss Pearmain, please don't do that."

She broke off to say, "Explain properly and I won't."

"The company, with assistance from providers, facilitators, and drivers, offers vouchers in several categories. Some of these vouchers are for tangible items, gifts or keepsakes, such as a bespoke gown or a new rose, or a one-of-a-kind piece of jewellery. They are *never* for something easily available via other means."

"No plush cats with diamanté collars or seed pearl brace-lets with pink enamel clasps, then."

"No — not unless or until someone requires us to recreate a lost treasure of that type."

Pip toyed with the idea of asking if a replacement diamanté collar could be provided for the first plush cat she'd received. That would test them!

Before she could phrase the request, Trip resumed his explanation.

"Most of the vouchers are for Experiences. Recipients are collected from their door by a V-S driver who takes them to a destination where the Experience can be facilitated and who returns them to the starting point afterwards."

"Semantics. How is that different from gift vouchers or a taxi or limo-service?" Pip asked.

Trip chuckled. "It's different because the Experiences and the destinations are mysteries. Whoever buys the voucher, whether for themselves or for someone else, makes general broad choices, according to funds and timeframe and desire. V-S tailors the Experience to match by using providers skilled in that area. Desires and dealbreakers can be specified, or the voucher can be left open to every eventuality."

"*Every* eventuality?"

"Well — with the caveat that we expect our clients to survive the Experience and to return home with their mental and physical health at least as good as when they left."

"So, no one will be ejected into space with ten hours of oxygen and collected twelve hours later, turning blue."

"Definitely not."

"Oh."

Trip said, gently, "You sound disappointed, Miss Pearmain."

"I'm not. It would be peaceful if the collection was made at nine hours, though. If that collection was guaranteed."

"What good would a guarantee be if you were in space?"

Pip said, "If I had a working phone, and I wasn't collected by nine hours on the dot, I *would* call to remind the collector of our deal."

Trip made no response, and the hypothetical situation was impossible anyway, so Pip continued. "What kind of dealbreaker are we talking?"

"If a recipient has two weeks of holiday leave, V-S will ensure the Experience fits inside that timeframe. It would be a poor return for the donor if the recipient spent a magical month on an offshore island but lost a job in consequence. It would contravene our *at least as good* policy.

"If a donor specifies that the recipient is—say—allergic to penguins, then a week observing a chin-strap colony in the Fijordlands would not be a suitable option.

"A tee-totaller or a recovering alcoholic wouldn't be sent for a relaxing wine-tasting tour in Provence.

"A—"

"That's enough peculiar examples," Pip said before he could continue. "My voucher doesn't say anything regarding dealbreakers."

"Miss de Leon left it wide open, allowing the company to make the choices for you."

Pip felt exasperated. As with so many people she'd dealt with over her sixty-six years, Trip gave her a great deal of information without telling her what she wanted to know.

She longed for Sully, who had always known what was important and who had never bothered her with what wasn't. She would tell Pip *anything* if she asked. That meant she didn't need to ask. Sully fixed things and they stayed fixed while Sully was in charge.

Now Sully was gone, they had a tendency to unravel. Cue the bank manager who had tried to deprive her of the benefits Sully had set in place.

Although, Pip allowed belatedly, presumably it wasn't the bank manager's fault, exactly. It would have come down to policy.

It was his fault for being patronising and having his gaze wander off to his phone. Unless he was contemplating calling his supervisor.

"Do you understand, Miss Pearmain?"

Pip jerked into focus. "What do I do to use the voucher? How do I set this in motion…or not?"

"It was activated as soon as I answered your call. All you need to do is to give your voucher to the driver who comes to collect you."

"For *what*?"

"For your Experience." He sighed. "Miss Pearmain, I normally wouldn't mention this, but I knew your cousin Lupin de Leon well. She worked in the company for a few years after her retirement from her original employment. Mary and I liked her very much. We considered her a friend and we were saddened to hear of her passing. We would be sorry if her gift to you should go to waste so please —"

Pip hummed.

"Miss Pearmain?"

"Hush, you. I'm counting on my fingers. Do I have to start *and* finish before the expiry date?"

"No, but once a voucher is activated, it's necessary —"

Fortunately, Pip had a deadline in mind already. She said, "I am expecting an important phone call from my new agent at eight o'clock in the morning a week from today. If I agree to the proposition she's put to me, I will have to fly interstate for a screen test in the near future."

"Then you will be returned to your pick-up point before eight o'clock on Monday morning," Trip said.

"I need to arrange someone to care for my housemates. They're cats."

Trip said, "Your driver will look after your cats. He has an affiliation with animals."

"But —"

Trip continued, "Write a list of instructions for him and give it, and your keys, to him when he arrives. I have known him since the day of his birth, and he is utterly trustworthy. I stake my life and reputation on that."

Pip heard an odd, musical sound that could have been spelled *Ker-chinga-ling-ba-ba-ka-ching!*

"What was that?"

"That was my deal-done-activation fanfare. Did you like it?"

"It sounded like something off a cheesy nineteen-eighties game show. The kind with smooth-faced hosts in suits and blonde hostesses in slinky pink gowns."

"Excellent. That was the effect I was going for. I have your address in the system. Pick up will be in fifty-nine minutes."

What?

"Wait — how did you get my address? I didn't — I can't possibly be ready —"

For the second time that afternoon, Pip heard dead air through her phone.

CHAPTER SEVEN. DON'T POKE THE LEMON

Pip couldn't remember being so floored since—well, since Sully went to glory, seated on Little Mum Rosie's brocade rocker.

Her lips trembled and she hummed so violently she felt the reverberation right through the soles of her feet.

When the angry blur in her vision eased, she became aware of three pairs of eyes gazing at her with fascination. Blue, amber and green—they shone with an eerie effect of not-quite-traffic-lights.

"What are you looking at?" she growled.

Miss Pippin Picotee Pearmain, getting her comeuppance, Kittisack signalled.

Pip ground her teeth. She thought it was a pity she hadn't thought to take a bite out of a Bushman's Best Biscuit first, because she would have easily reduced it to powder.

"I won't go," she said.

Amberjill purred soothingly. *Think of the benefits.*

If you don't go, you'll be wasting Lupin's last gift, Lupin's cat reproached.

"So—you think it's okay for her to manipulate *me* with lemon juice messages and madmen called Trip? And, forsooth, to do it from beyond the bucket she kicked when I can't—" Her voice choked with indignation.

The original cat and the back-up cat exchanged slow blinks.

Lupin's cat said, *Come on Tiny Pippin Pearmain — where's your sense of adventure?*

"I never had one," Pip said. "Are you aware that you sound a lot like Lupin?"

I was unaware, but it is meet that it be so. I was blessed by a guardian, and he held her hand as she stepped forth to glory.

Pip felt her eyes glaze, this time with indignation. Pottery cats, no matter how cockeyed, had no need to start sounding biblical.

Better start those instructions, signalled Kittisack, between dabs of his tongue as he groomed his underpinnings.

We need to be fed, Amberjill added, bringing the weirdest conversation of Pip's life firmly down to earth.

Sulkily, Pip got out her bucket list and snapped off the green pen that held the pages together.

She hunted down an old exercise book containing a rough-draft piece of choreography for a ballet that would never happen, ripped out the fading pages and wrote a practical heading in her tiny lettering.

Instructions for Cat Care etc. at Lemonwood Cottage

She underlined it three times and drew some curlicues and a set of fine cats' whiskers.

Get on with it, the original cat ordered.

Pip sneered her lip at him.

She drew a figure one and embellished it with climbing ivy. She added a lemon on top.

After that, she wrote — *Cats present. Cat One — the original cat — is the Siamese tommie. Cat Two — the back-up cat — is the tortoiseshell queen.*

She paused to consider.

I will leave a fresh pack of chicken-and-rice in the fridge. Feed the cats on the porch using the bowls by the door. Half a cup of food each, at nine in the morning. Wash bowls after use.

A few small cubes of cheese may be given as treats later in the day. Make sure the water bowl, also on the porch, is kept full.

Otherwise the cats are self-sufficient.

She glanced at Lupin's cat. "I can't add you to the cat list. This person would think I was daft."

She wrote a neat figure two and decorated it with camomile flowers and a gooseberry.

The Cottage.

I have made up the bed with clean linen.

She hadn't but she would.

Help yourself to food in the fridge, freezer or pantry, or from the garden.

Lock the door if you leave the cottage and garden during the day or night and remember to take the key with you. Do not put it under a flowerpot or hang it on the nail beside the door.

The TV remote control is on the table.

It wasn't yet, but it would be.

Spare batteries are in the top drawer in the kitchen cabinet. Dispose of the used ones in the cracked teapot on the top shelf. There is a step-stool if you need it. Do not use that pot to make tea.

She recalled a shocking experience with a volunteer gardener and penned a figure three. She gave that one cats' ears.

The Garden.

The tall daisies in the garden are camomile and are not weeds. Do not prune, mow or uproot them.

More vigorous underlining made her point on that.

This cottage is on tank supply. Water is not unlimited. If you have a lot of hair, turn the shower off while the conditioner is working. If you use that sort of conditioner. I recommend Caraway's Comfort Glossy Locks. Use the camomile one if you are blond. The Indian Tea one works if you happen to be dark. Neither of them needs to be rinsed out.

The blue-tongue who lives in the woodheap is called Bill. He cares for himself. He is friendly. He enjoys tomatoes.

The gooseberry bush by the tank is not friendly. Avoid it.

The lemon tree near it is especially not friendly. I suspect they collude.

She underlined that bit three times as well.

Stay well clear unless you want to use lemons. If you do, be aware they will —

Her phone chimed.

Pip opened the message.

V-S e.t.a. 35 mins.

What?

Hurriedly, Pip wrote *Don't poke the lemons* in capital letters. She added, *If you must poke the lemons put on my onion goggles first. They are on the table.*

They weren't, but they would be.

She put down the instructions.

Did you tell him where the cheese is kept? Amberjill wanted to know.

"He'll find it."

Pip removed a new pack of cat fodder from the freezer and put it in the fridge. She headed for the bedroom where she stripped and changed the bedding.

She folded three clean towels on the foot of the bed, found the TV remote and her onion goggles and put them on the kitchen table, along with her rubber gloves. The driver's hands would be bigger than hers, but the gloves were over-sized on her anyway.

She checked for embarrassing items and decided her houseguest, whoever he was, would just have to put up with her favourite cat-paw socks and the collection of beetle cases and porcelain shoes with Jellico diamonds in them on the mantelpiece beyond the candlesticks and Lupin's cat.

The embarrassing plush cats with their diamanté collars were still in the taped-up boxes they'd occupied since her move to Jellico Bay. The seed pearl bracelets were with them, securely out of sight. They weren't embarrassing in the singular, she supposed, but so many of them hinted at an obsession she didn't have.

The lacy bikini knickers draped over the airing rail along

with her A-cup bras were probably an eyesore to delicate male sensibilities.

She bundled them into the under-bed drawer.

If he snoops in there he deserves to be bitten by knickers or ambushed by a winter woollen vest.

As she fussed around she pondered how odd it was. When she used to travel regularly for work, Sully had arranged the travel and itinerary. She'd had an always-packed bag to take to film sets and rehearsal venues. Little Mum had taken care of whatever was needed at home while Pip was away, so she had never before needed to leave someone a list of *things to do.*

In *Treasures*, the old family home in Delmsford, there had been half a century of amiable animals for love and company, but they had never depended on Pip's permanent presence. By the time she sold the house and flitted, natural attrition ensured they had all completed their days in Little Mum's care. The last one, the grey cat called Duster, had gone into his final sleep on the same day as Little Mum.

Pip's eyes had been sore from weeping for Little Mum...and then Duster elicited a few more regretful tears. Next went Sully three days later, passing into glory in her mad black comedy way in the middle of a scurrilous story...

She whirled to face the original cat. "Why are you in such a hurry to get me out of the cottage?"

The cat licked a paw in a don't-care fashion.

"Amberjill? Not long ago, you were worried about Lupin's cat disrupting your routine. Now you're happy to see me go off disrupting you *twice.* Why?"

The calico patted a stray piece of sticky tape with her front left paw.

Lupin's cat signalled *I am here to watch over them.*

"I know you are—oh, I give up."

Pip switched on the kettle and prepped a cup of camomile tea.

The mobile chimed again.
V-S e.t.a. 10 mins.
Pip slammed her hands over her cheeks.
I haven't packed yet!
She dashed into the bedroom.

Opening the wardrobe solved nothing. Her dancing costumes hung to the side of her ordinary clothes with her shoes set neatly underneath.
Books?
No time to choose.
Pip took a big breath in.
Messenger bag.

In it were her wallet, a comb, her favourite Caraway's Comfits, a handkerchief, and Sully's tektite heaven and earth ring, enclosed in its wee drawstring bag and pinned securely to the lining. Her bucket list was there, with its familiar green pen which she must have automatically re-clipped after writing the note.
Breathe.

She detached her phone charger from the power board by the bed and zipped it into the bag.

She rescued a spare pair of knickers, a long T-shirt, and some socks from the under-bed drawer and dropped them into the side-pouch where they made an annoying bulge. She relocated the T-shirt to the main part of the bag.
Toothbrush!

It had seen better days, but she took it anyway, along with a bar of her favourite Caraway's Comforts soap, a bottle of *Loving Lotion,* and a sample-sized tube of toothpaste that must have been in her cupboard almost since the flit.
Phone.

She retrieved it from the kitchen table just as it chimed with another message.
V-S e.t.a. 1 min.

Breathlessly, Pip opened the fridge and got out the cheese.

She cut nine small cubes and hesitated.

I can't give any to Lupin's cat. That's too daft, even for me...shades of offerings to the golden calf...it'd melt or mummify and attract ants.

She squinted across at the mantelpiece. "You don't require any of this cheese — do you?"

Thank you for the thought, dear mistress. I am not a consumer of cheese.

She heard a car pull up outside.

She glanced at her special favourite cup, wreathed with marigolds.

I should put it away. But Trip said the driver was utterly trustworthy... and I'm leaving him with the cats...

The marigold cup could stay on its special shelf.

CHAPTER EIGHT. NOT THE NAPPING SORT

"Okay." Pip scooped up Kittisack. "Behave yourself, right?"

The tip of the original cat's tail informed her of his displeasure at being picked up without a by-your-leave. Pip put him down with four pieces of cheese for mollification.

She ran a finger over the back-up cat's head. "Amberjill, be good."

The calico gave her a winsome blink and hooked a piece of cheese with her claw.

Pip said, "Lupin's cat, keep them under control. Don't let them terrorise Bill or—"

Someone knocked on the door.

All will be well.

Pip stuck the last piece of cheese in her mouth and chewed. She cast a wistful glance at the camomile tea she'd prepped but not poured.

She briefly pondered the jeans and the green boys' shirt she had on with her daisy-toed shoes.

Then she opened the door.

Outside stood a lanky but *very* young man with shaggy light-brown hair and hazel eyes. "Hi."

As usual when strangers met Pip, his chin dropped abruptly as he relocated his gaze from above her head to her face.

Pip said, "You're too young to be a driver."

"Gerry taught me to drive when I was twelve. I have six years of experience and a valid licence." He tapped his shirt, which was a conservative denim blue with a paler blue V-S monogram on it. He added, "My name's Jamie. That's all I'm allowed to tell you."

"Are you the person who's going to mind the cats while I'm away?"

He looked perplexed.

"Don't say you don't know there are cats. I won't go anywhere unless I can be sure they'll be properly cared for."

"It's not that. I like cats and they generally like me. I know how to care for them. This is not my first association with cats. You might say I'm the cat specialist."

"Enough! Were you told these cats are used to company? Do you know they need someone *here*, not just a five-minute daily visit with kibble?"

He jumped. "I don't know if this comes under the banner of things I can't tell you."

"Tell me, or I'm going nowhere." Pip folded her arms and tilted her chin so she could fix him with her most menacing gaze.

The un-poured camomile tea enticed her to cut her losses and stay at home.

This driver looked far too young, like a leggy adolescent pup, but he was tidy. He smelled of something pleasant—she thought it might have been pears. He was much taller than Pip—most people were—but there was something in him that reminded her of herself.

Maybe it was the set of his ears, or the way he seemed to be listening to music in his mind. He looked as if he knew the way he appeared and was comfortable with it.

She glanced at his hands. One fingertip was stained with green ink, and he had a neatly-healed scar on the back of his left hand. It didn't look like a cat scratch. He didn't bite his nails.

"Is this your first job, by any chance?" she asked suspiciously, recalling a green taxi driver in Melbourne who had expected *her* to navigate.

She supposed that wouldn't happen now. They all had maps on their phones or those onboard car computer monitors.

He sidestepped the question. "Have you written out instructions for me? I was told you'd give me some."

She thrust the exercise book forward. "Here." She unhooked the cottage key from her Butterfly Princess keyring and gave him that, too.

He opened the book and glanced down the first green-penned lines. His eyebrows rose a fraction as he took in the tiny writing.

"Angels on the head of a pin?" he enquired.

"I've never seen an angel capering around on my notes."

He blinked, and visibly refocused his eyes to read a little way.

"There was no need to make up the bed for me, Miss Pearmain. I brought my own. Gerry should have told —"

"What?"

Pip looked around. "Oh — you have one of those portable swag things?" She'd had one of those while filming *Dingo Nights* in 2004. She'd played Tanner, the fiercely independent protagonist who, stalked by a killer, had elected to *go bush* and lose herself. She'd liked that swag. It had been cosy. She'd liked the role, too. It might have been a breakout role, with its vast outback skyscapes and its enigmatic ending, but instead, it was the last mainstream film she'd been in.

"Something like that. I can curl up in it." Jamie closed the book and dropped it on the porch swing. "I'll pick it up when I come back, and I will take notice of it," he assured her. "If it's in the car with me I'll be itching to read it." He gave her a confiding grin. "I'll read *anything*."

"I won't. I never read anything I don't want to read unless someone's paying me." Pip locked the door by pulling it closed with its familiar *clu-unk.*

"You have to make sure you get the *unk* after the *clu*, because otherwise the lock doesn't engage properly," she said.

"*Clu-unk.* Gotcha."

Her driver put the key into his shirt pocket and engaged the button to keep it safe. He indicated a blue station wagon with the V-S logo on the door. It was parked where Jan's car had recently been.

It was bigger than Jan's vehicle. However had he got it through the gate?

He stepped down from the porch and opened the rear passenger door. "In you get, Miss Pearmain...um...that is who you are? I should have checked, though you'd probably have said you weren't by now if you were someone else."

"That's who I am."

Pip got into the back of the vehicle and clicked up her seatbelt. "Where are we going?"

"I'm not allowed to tell you."

"Is it far?"

"I'm not—"

"Stop that! I have to know because I don't want the cats left alone too long. They're independent, but they are used to having me here."

"They won't be alone for long. I'll be back here within— not long. Do your cats get along with dogs?"

Pip had no idea, so she prevaricated. "What kind of dogs? Big dogs? Chi-dogs? Beagle-dogs? Heeler-dogs?"

Jamie sucked in his bottom lip, bent and held his hand out at knee-height. "Poodlish-dogs. Around this big."

"Possibly. Why? Do you have some?"

"Sort of. Not exactly. Not dogs in plural. He's a good dog.

Not vicious. Respectable." He squirmed.

"I need your word that the not-vicious dog you sort of and not exactly have won't traumatise the cats—or Bill blue-tongue."

"I can promise you that. It might go the other way. He's been known to be timorous when faced with fangs."

"He may cock his leg on the lemon tree if he's prepared to take the consequences, but *not*, repeat *not*, on the camomile."

He bobbed his head, grinning. He probably thought she was joking.

She wasn't.

"I need to see your voucher."

She handed it over. He took a self-inking stamp from his jeans' pocket and slapped it down on the voucher.

"And another thing—" Pip began.

The door snapped closed.

Jamie got into the driver's seat. He caught Pip's gaze in the rear-view mirror. "Make yourself comfortable. There's music, and magazines, books, tea and coffee, bottled water, snacks... You could have a nap—oh, no. I can see you're not the napping sort."

Before Pip could respond, he had engaged some sort of switch, and a smoked-glass panel rose from behind the front seats so all she saw was an underwater blur.

When she tried to look out the window, she realised the glass was tinted from the inside out.

She was cocooned.

Part Two. Making Waves

CHAPTER ONE. TULPENMANIE

It felt odd, being driven and unable to see outside. Pip soon lost her sense of direction.

She made a few efforts to engage Jamie in conversation, but she eventually realised he couldn't hear her.

He's kidnapped me. A lovely young man has kidnapped me. Must tell Juniper Gin!

She felt for her Pink Princess phone. Jan might be still driving—she had lost track of time—but she could leave a message.

She hit Jan's number which her phone had thoughtfully saved for her.

Instead of beginning an obliging ringing pattern, the phone informed her stuffily that the mobile she was calling was out of service—or possibly Pip was. It recommended calling again, but it didn't sound convinced that the luck would be better if she did.

Hmph.

All kidnapped up and no one to boast to.

Okay, so that was in poor taste, because some poor souls *did* get kidnapped and some of them came to harm. Still, if Jamie meant her any harm, she would eat the V-S car and follow it up with Lupin's cat's tape-and-tissue mummy wrappings for dessert.

She reflected that the last people to kidnap her had been Lupin and Jan, back in February. They hadn't meant her any harm either, but the disruption of that afternoon tea was still twanging in her psyche.

After a bit, Pip took out her bucket list and cruised through some entries. She intended to make a new one, but to her annoyance she had no remembered buckets to add.

I can't have written them all up yet.

The thought brought mild panic. Sometimes she went weeks between making additions to her list, but it was always there in the back of her mind as a pleasurable possibility.

Wait, didn't Sully have a dedicated ash bucket for her stove? It was grey-silver, and it had Ashses to Ashes on the side in permanent ink. She used to say she wished her lipstick would stay on as well as permanently-inked errors did.

Pip flicked through pages and discovered that yes, Sully had definitely had that bucket. There was a catch, though — the ash bucket had already been entered as number 51.

She penned in a careful ellipsis on a new page. Lupin had said no one knew the future, and an ellipsis meant the bucket list wasn't dead yet. She put away the feint-ruled pad. This *wasn't* the end. Another bucket *would* come to mind. If not, she'd be bound to see a new one — maybe today!

It was so quiet. She couldn't even hear the car's purr. It must be quieter than the original cat's.

Kittisack? Amberjill? Lupin's cat?

Silence. How could they hear her from so far away?

Pip began to hum.

She was still humming when the car stopped.

A few seconds passed, and the back of Jamie's head, blurred and fuzzy, shifted out of view.

The passenger door opened, and Pip looked up at him, widening her eyes as she used to do when she was first billed as *Tiny* Pippin Pearmain.

"Are we there yet?" she asked in a childish voice.

He grinned at her. "Sort of. First stage, anyhow. Miss Pearmain, are you the kind of woman who enjoys being assisted out of cars?"

"What do you think?"

"Probably no. Possibly at my own peril."

Pip slid out of the car. She rose on tiptoe and raised her arms in a ballet curve. She danced the opening salvo to Drozdov's *Volny na Beregu*.

"*Waves on the Shore*... Just getting the kinks out," she said. She drove occasionally, but she wasn't much used to being a passenger.

Jamie seemed curiously unsurprised, nodding as if he knew that dance...although it seemed unlikely. "When you're finished your wave salutation, I'll hand you on to the next — um — provider."

"You're not taking me all the way?" Pip made the fluttering run that should have ushered in the larger waves and dropped a sweeping curtsey, a *grand reverence* to the ocean.

He bowed, deadpan, offering his hand. "No. Apparently I have cats to mind. However, I will hand you safely on to the next part of your journey."

Pip took his hand briefly, came upright, and looked around curiously. She didn't know where they were, but it was obviously somewhere on the coast. She saw a long level beach and smelled brine.

No wonder that was the dance that came to mind. I wonder if there are Jellico diamonds here, or something like them.

Out to sea she saw a sailing ship — a yacht. It had multicoloured sails. Two people were lowering a dinghy over the side in some kind of sling contraption.

"We're a bit early for the rendezvous," Jamie observed.

"You can go if you like."

"I prefer to stay. You look like a slippery person, and I want to make sure you don't vanish before you're collected. We're not supposed to let our voucherfolk escape. Questions might be asked."

"Pretty," Pip remarked, gazing at the yacht. "What's her name?"

"I'm not supposed to say."

"If I had binoculars I could read it."

He shrugged and handed her some.

Huh? He carries binoculars in his pocket?

Pip unclipped the lids and raised the binoculars to her eyes, twiddling to fix the focus. "*Tulpenmanie.*" She shifted the angle and caught a brief glimpse of a man with curly blond hair and a dark-haired woman.

Jamie took the binoculars back without fuss and without asking.

"She's skippered by a couple named Bart and Brigitta, but I think you won't be seeing them today."

"Am I going to learn to sail, then?"

Maybe Lupin thought that would be a good idea . . .but then, Lupin thought making pottery in Adelaide would be a good idea.

"I don't know. I'm just the driver."

"I like you, Jamie. You're at least as slippery as I am."

"So my sister says."

"What's her name?"

"Laura. Ah!"

The two people who had been superintending the dinghy straightened. A third person moved into view, and they seemed to be having a dispute. The newcomer was bare-chested and wearing — what?

Oo-la-la!

"Oh," Jamie said.

"Oh what?"

Jamie whistled gently between his teeth.

"Jamie."

He stopped. "Just *oh.* I was hoping it might be someone else playing third hand, but you're going to have to deal with my uncle."

"What's wrong with him?" Pip asked suspiciously. She'd never had a proper uncle, only Lupin and Jan's dad, Lance de Leon, who was married to Pip's Aunt Helen.

"Not a thing. I love him. We all do. He's just — different."

One of the three people, the man with blond hair, climbed down a rope ladder into the dinghy. He cast off and started a motor with a single pull.

Jamie sighed. "At least you're meeting the user-friendly one first."

Pip wanted to ask more, but she stood silently watching the dinghy approach.

The motor cut out and the dinghy lost way and began to toss in the light waves.

"Jamie, can you haul me in?" the blond man called.

"If you chuck me the rope."

The blond picked up a coiled rope and tossed it casually forth.

Jamie caught it without apparently looking.

He pulled.

The boat glided forward and beached gently on the sand.

Jamie said, "Zach, this is Miss Pippin Pearmain."

The man called Zach looked mildly disconcerted. "But she's—"

"Smaller and older than you expected," Pip supplied, beaming at him. She enjoyed disconcerting people.

"She'll be fine," Jamie said. "Up for anything, right, Miss Pearmain?"

Pip definitely wasn't, but she had taken a liking to Jamie, and she wanted his approval. She smiled up at him and nodded mendaciously. "I'll see you when you come to pick me up," she said.

"Yes. I'd better go now. Cats are waiting."

Zach reached out as if to detain him. "Help her in before you run off, would you?"

Jamie asked, "Miss Pearmain, are you the sort of lady who likes being helped into boats?"

Oh, so I'm a lady now. Interesting development.

"On the whole, yes. In fact, you might lift me in and deposit me nicely on the seat." Pip reached up, smiling, exactly as she had when she was being The Dorothy in *Ruby Shoes Emporium.*

She didn't expect Jamie to have seen that relic of the late 1970s, but surely he knew how to lift a very small lady into a boat without pinching bits of her on the way.

Her faith was vindicated.

Chapter Two. Rat on a Mission

Pip settled in the stern of the dinghy. She remembered all the terminology from being the unseen leprechaun in *Shamrock Sailors* back in 1966.

Funny how things she'd learned for roles often stuck with her.

If only she could recall the name of that first play, the one with the Greeks that had started it all! Not *The Dream*, or *The Tempest*, she thought, and nothing to do with Socrates or Odysseus or even Icarus, but it had surely had Greeks in it.

If she could only ask one of the others from the cast…but it was almost sixty years ago and most of them would be long gone. Even the young lovers, Meleta and Tercus, if those had really been their names, would be well into their eighties by now.

You could look it up on the Internet. Search for Meleta and Tercus. The title might pop right up.

What's the fun in that?

She waved at Jamie in a queenly fashion. "Off you go. Remember—make sure the dog you sort of have doesn't pee on my camomile or bother Bill blue-tongue and *watch out for that lemon tree*."

Jamie ducked his head, grinning. Pip heard the other man, Zach, make a strange choking sound just before Jamie reached out one foot and gave the dinghy a hearty shove.

The dinghy rocked.

Zach started the engine, then throttled it down to a putter. He turned to face Pip. "Kids, eh?"

Pip beamed at him. "He's *yours*?" She clasped her hands.

That was pure provocation, since Zach looked little more than thirty.

"He's not mine. Not in any sense."

"Just how old is he?"

Zach said gently, "I'm sure you've been told we can't answer questions."

"And I'm sure *you've* been told to be polite to your elders. How old is he? He sort of said, mathematically, but I want to be sure he's legally able to drive a car, vote and drink alcohol—though *not* when driving a car."

"Eighteen or so—I think—and terrifically legal." Zach watched as Jamie returned to the V-S vehicle and drove away. "Why? Were you going to ply him with strong drink? I warn you—it wouldn't have much effect."

"The strongest thing I ply people with is camomile tea, but he's going to look after the cats and the cottage while I have an Experience. Therefore, I need him to be competent. And sober."

"I'm sure he is. His mother is fearfully competent." Zach passed a hand over his blond curls. He looked worried. "Miss Pearmain, I don't know how much you've been told regarding your voucher."

"Almost nothing. Since it was a present, I should have got to choose how to spend it, but the person on the phone railroaded me."

"I expect he thought you needed some motivation. Can you keep your mouth shut under interrogation, Miss Pearmain?"

"Not a chance. One sight of a pair of pruners or some toothpicks heading for my toes, and I'll sing like a green canary."

"Not that sort of interrogation. I mean—if Gerry Trip asks you what you were told and by whom—"

"Silent as the sphinx."

"That's what I thought. I don't work for him, by the way. I'm not a V-S employee. However, I crew for the owners of *Tulpenmanie*, and Gerry needed *someone* who knew what he was doing at sea and who was licensed to do it. You see, I've known—"

"I don't need your autobiography," Pip said.

He looked relieved.

"Just tell me the relevant bits so I have less to plausibly deny."

"Okay. You're booked for an Experience. I didn't tell you this but—"

Pip growled.

"It *will* involve *Tulpenmanie,* but it *might* involve something rather—"

"Dangerous?" She didn't *do* danger.

"No! Not really. Not a bit. Although you might perceive it that way. You'll be offered a chance at that *extra* experience at some point, but you do *not* have to say yes. Get it? You can say *no*, politely, and that will be that."

"And I then get put ashore as punishment."

"No, you'll get a lovely cruise, good food, ocean scenery and some possibly interesting and probably peculiar conversation."

Pip frowned. "If you'd asked me yesterday, I'd have said a cruise was not on my lists of things to do this week."

"Well—I can't tell you more because I don't know more. However, my girlfriend and Jamie's uncle are the other people crewing, and when those two get together, all bets are off."

"Jamie said you were the user-friendly option aboard."

He didn't look gratified.

"What did he mean?" Pip pressed.

"Well, I'm human for a start!"

"That's no recommendation and no distinction. So am I."

He gave her a straight look. "You sound unnerved. Do you

want me to put you ashore?"

Pip gave it some thought. Jamie had gone, but she could call a taxi and go home to finish making her camomile tea. She had ballet practice to do in the morning, and cats to mind, a lemon tree to battle and replacement tarts to buy…and yet, if all went to plan her life would be disrupted at eight o'clock on Monday next, so why not play *this* role and see where it took her? Things had been mildly off-key since the flower show. Besides, Sully had been solid on seeing things through.

"I'll stay. Wouldn't want to get you into trouble with what's his name—Trip."

"He's not my boss, remember. Even if he was, I wouldn't be scared." He gave her a head-ducking grin that reminded her of Jamie's. "It takes a lot to scare a man in my profession."

"You're black ops?" she asked politely.

"Much tougher gig than that." He leaned forward. "I teach five-year-olds."

Pip laughed.

"I'm serious." Zach took out a PFD from under the seat. "It might be a bit big."

Pip put it on. It was a *lot* big.

She wished Jan was there with the bread knife to saw it down to size. She'd made such a good job of cutting the tissue-and-sticky-tape mummy wrappings away to reveal Lupin's cat.

The dinghy puttered back to *Tulpenmanie*.

The woman Pip had seen from the shore watched the approach with a deadpan expression. She had long dark hair, and there was something odd about her eyes.

Cat's eyes. The message sounded like Kittisack, but he couldn't possibly be there.

Pip looked up into those brilliant eyes as the dinghy bumped gently into the yacht. One eye was blue, and one was green—not just variations on grey or hazel, but clear, true colours of blue sapphire and peridot.

And I thought I was odd…

She smiled.

The woman didn't.

She looked past Pip and said, in a cool and reasonable tone, "How do you expect her to get aboard?"

Zach gave her a chiding look. "Play nicely, Jin. Use your inside voice."

The woman said, "Just you wait."

Pip said, *"Gin?"*

The mismatched eyes swivelled in her direction in a feline fashion. "Jin. With a Jay. Why not?"

"My cousin is Juniper Gin. Gin with a Gee. She writes bodice rippers."

Up went neat black brows. "Would I like them?"

"I do." She added, "I can climb a rope, you know."

"Really?" Jin-with-a-J sounded doubtful.

"Really. One of my press cuttings said *Tiny Pippin Pearmain shot up the rope like a rat on a mission.* I always liked that reviewer. He didn't say I was *cute.*"

Jin's incredulous gaze switched over Pip's shoulder to Zach. "Is this one quite sane, do you think?"

Pip said, "I've often wondered that myself. Have you ever heard of Cat-Morse, Jin-with-a-Jay?"

Click. The gemstone gaze snapped back to her face.

"Never."

Zach said, tolerantly, "If you've finished posturing, Jisinia-mine… Let down the ladder. Why did you pull it up, anyway?"

"I didn't. Tane did."

"Why did you let him?"

Jin pouted at him. "You're no fun."

"Jisinia. Is that a flower name?" Pip asked.

Click. Jin's gaze had reconnected. "Yes, it's Spanish."

"You're not, though."

"No. How did you know the origin of my name?"

Pip said, "My family is into plant names. Little Nanna Pearmain was called Schizanthus. Can you spell that?"

"No." Jin stepped back from the rail and bundled a rope ladder over. It tumbled like Rapunzel's braid and pooled in the bottom of the dinghy.

"Neither can I," Pip confided. "Not being able to spell words like that got me sacked from minute-taking for the Delmsford Flower Club Committee in nineteen seventy-two." She eyed the ladder. The rungs were made of rope rather than wood, so the thing would be unstable.

Quick and agile. Never stand on a rung long enough for it to sag and grab your shoe or turn your ankle.

She got to her feet and stepped up on the seat before grabbing the ladder in both hands.

One foot...go!

Up she went. It was like riding a bike — almost — except that it was no longer 1966, she was no longer eleven and she was wearing an over-sized PFD.

Still, Pip managed it, arriving at the top before the startled Jin could jump back.

Pip leaned over, transferring her grip to the rail. "*Boo!*"

Jin said, "Cat-Morse?" in a questioning tone.

CHAPTER THREE. CHARTED WATERS

Pip decided she quite liked Jin-with-a-J, but it was disappointing that she had never heard of Cat-Morse. It was true that no one else had ever mentioned knowing it, but she'd hoped it was one of those things that folk didn't mention...like having chalky deposits under their toenails.

"Never mind," she said.

Getting over the rail was a little difficult, but she blamed the PFD.

Presently she made it to the deck, and that seemed to be that.

Now what?

She'd been on a ship before, but that one had been part of a film-set. The script and the director had the sequence all planned out and the acting coach was ready to pick up the slack.

Not that Pip had ever needed her.

She'd been a performer for decades, but she had never been the sort to talk of *My Art* or to attend champagne parties on yachts. She didn't think what she did was *Art*. It was just what she did. Sully had been firm regarding that, and equally firm about the parties. Sully loved a beer or three, especially a brew called Fagus Ale, but when Pip turned eighteen, Sully explained what she called an algorithm of units of alcohol per kilogram of body weight. She'd told Pip that although she was of legal drinking age she would have to be much more careful of her intake than her larger peers.

The world does not need one more news item passing on gossip and lamenting a child star gone wrong.

Bad for you. Bad for me. Bad for the agency.

Little Mum Rosie had corroborated the information on units and kilograms, as had both Little Nannas and Aunt Helen.

The Little Nannas suggested shandies, and heavy on the lemon.

Big Nanna de Leon, who could remove bottle caps with her teeth and neck three beers without drawing breath, had given a tolerant shrug and said, *Shandies are for pussies, but better safe than sorry, Pippsi-Pola.*

Pip glanced up. In *Shamrock Sailors* she'd gone up the rope, over the rail, swarmed into the rigging and settled in the crows' nest, but it would look affected if she did that now. Besides, *Tulpenmanie* didn't have a crow.

"Can I take this off?" she asked Jin, tugging at the PFD. It came down her legs and interrupted her elbows.

"Sorry, regulations say you need to keep it on."

Jin didn't sound sorry.

"Can I at least have one that fits? I feel like Tom Kitten in the roly-poly pudding."

A glitch of a grin warmed Jin's eyes.

She might not know Cat-Morse, but she knew the story of Tom Kitten.

"With your little paws sticking out and the rats sharpening the cutlery...I'll see what I can find."

Jin walked away across the deck and vanished down a companionway.

Pip wondered if she knew the book called *Grandmother's Sunshine* too. In all her life she'd never met *anyone* outside her family who'd heard of *Grandmother's Sunshine*. She had one copy, inherited from Little Mum.

Lupin and Jan had another. That one had belonged to Aunt Helen de Leon. Since Lupin went to glory, that copy was Jan's alone.

Zach arrived at the top of the rail and sprang over to land on his toes.

"Winch!" he yelled.

A motor whirred, and Pip looked over the side in time to see the dinghy rising like a spider on a thread.

"You could have let me stay in the boat and come up like a lady in a sedan chair," she told Zach.

"That's against regulations."

"What, like not being allowed to sleep in a caravan under tow?"

She'd always wanted to do that, ever since she played Walnut Wednesday in *Gypsy Summer*. Though, come to think of it, the caravan, or *varda* in which she rode, wasn't exactly under tow. It was pulled by a patient chestnut horse named Evadne.

"More or less," Zach said.

Jin emerged from the companionway bearing an emerald-green PFD. "This belongs to my cousin Cèilidh," she informed Pip. "Don't damage it or she'll hex you."

"She's a witch?" Pip was impressed, but not especially surprised. She'd often had her suspicions of Little Nanna Laurel who always knew when someone was telling fibs and who could bully warts away with raw beef and sheer force of personality.

Jin said, "No, she's a barmaid."

"Is she big enough?" Pip removed the elbow interrupter and put on the green affair, which fitted perfectly.

"More or less," Jin said drily.

"She stands on a milking stool if necessary," Zach said.

Pip almost remarked that it was odd that Cèilidh should be so small, if Jisinia was her cousin, but then she recalled that Jin was around the same size as Lupin.

Lupin. The pain of loss was curiously distant. She was enjoying Lupin's last gift to her rather a lot, but none of it so far had the *feel* of Lupin. Lupin might have persuaded Jan to go to Adelaide where they took a pottery class, but she couldn't imagine Lupin on a sailing ship—ever.

People don't change.

Maybe Lupin was secretly not the way she seemed.

Maybe Headmistress and Senior Cousin were roles she inhabited as Pip had always inhabited the role of Tiny Pippin Pearmain.

I wish I could ask her.

She looked up at Jin. "Where are we going?"

She expected prevarication, but Jin said, "Zach has a chart. He'll show you, and you can choose where we sail to, within reason. *Tulpenmanie* is a sea-going yacht, but I think you have a deadline, so we can't go too far out."

"I have to be home by eight o'clock on Monday morning for work." It felt odd to say that, after a decade of increasing belief that the work had dried up forever. And maybe it had. The abrupt Magda Saxer had suggested she was up for a role, not that she had it in the bag. She'd be sent for a screen test.

It was years since Pip had a screen test. Her roles had often been written with her in mind. She was niche-market, but there was almost no one else to fill that niche.

She remembered screen tests in the 1960s. Sully and Little Mum used to go with her. It was *Let's Pretend* with a side helping of waiting around—and that used to be filled with stories, and drawing, and sometimes with schoolwork. And the older actors used to think she was a quaint little thing. They were always kind to her. Maybe they'd liked her. Maybe they'd just been covering their backs. No grown-up star wanted to be mean to Tiny Pippin Pearmain. It was not, in modern terms, a very good look.

Then there had been the hotbed friendships Sully had explained to her.

So they're not real? She'd struggled to understand.

They're real at the time, Pippin.

But you said they don't last.

Flowers don't last either, but that doesn't make them not-real while you have them.

If she went for this screen test, it would be her first without Sully.

Fancy having a working first at the age of sixty-six!

"Six days afloat, then," Jin said, looking over Pip's shoulder.

"I didn't bring enough luggage for that," Pip recalled belatedly, snapping out of her past. "No one told me I'd be going on a yacht. Usually if I need extra clothes or food I go to the shop—or someone does it for me if I'm stuck on set without transport."

"V-S vouchers come fully catered. Everything within reason is provided," Zach said in a reassuring tone.

"Even spare knickers in my size?"

"Yes, but I suppose you have some in that messenger bag. You look like a spare-socks-and-knickers person to me."

"If you're trying to shock him by mentioning your knickers, don't bother. He teaches five-year-olds," Jin drawled.

Pip grinned. "I don't ever wear old-lady knickers," she confided.

"Neither do I," Jin said.

"I'll show you the chart." Zach put paid to what might have been an interesting discussion upon underwear. Pip had been going to ask what Jin did wear, but probably she had better not. *She* always wore nice knickers. Little Nanna Pearmain had insisted on that. If a lady was going to get knocked over in the street, she'd better have on nice knickers. Even if she didn't get knocked down, the wind might blow up. Even if the day was calm, knickers should still be nice.

Nice things give a lady confidence, even if they're not on show.

Pip had almost always found the things the Little Nannas said were true. They were old-fashioned even then, but being old-fashioned didn't make them any less true.

Treat your hands and feet well. Rub Caraway lotions into your face. Don't mess with your hair. Wash it, condition it with Caraway's Glossy Locks, dry it and leave it be.

Have nice things. Don't wait for other people to give them to you. Give them to yourself.

Sometimes Pip thought she ought to write down the things the Little Nannas had said, but she thought a lot of them came from a book called *Herbal Lore* whose author was identified only by a set of initials, so probably somebody already had.

Zach went on, "Come down the companionway, Miss Pearmain. That's—"

"The stairs or ladder leading into the guts of a ship," Pip supplied glibly.

Jin clicked her tongue. "Don't you underestimate this one, Zach. She eats curly little lads like you for supper and picks her teeth with their bones."

"So do you," Zach said.

"Yum-yum." Jin laughed and blew him a kiss.

Pip asked, "Do you like cats, Zach?"

He looked surprised. "Yes. Why?"

"I thought you must. I do too. Remind me to tell you about the ones I live with—or get Jamie to do it. He's looking after them while I have my Experience. I hope—"

"Jamie is good with animals," Zach said.

Jisinia snickered silently.

"Ja? *Und?*" Pip said.

Jisinia looked startled at being caught up.

Pip gave her a quick stare then followed Zach down into a comfortable lounge area. It had swags and mattresses, sea chests, and a well-appointed galley.

"This is the chartroom." Zach took an enormous book out of one of the chests and laid it on a table that appeared to be bolted to the floor.

He motioned to Pip to sit beside him on the low seating and opened the book, using both hands to lift the cover.

"Proper charts," Pip observed. She traced some whorls that looked like contour lines.

"You can read them?" He sounded respectful.

"I can't, but they look real."

Zach said, "They are real, and pretty old, which means they're not altogether accurate. Bart — *Tulpenmanie's* owner and usual skipper — adapts in his head when he uses them. Obviously, he has all the modern state-of-the-art navigation gear too."

"Obviously," Pip said. It seemed equally obvious that Bart didn't use it often. *She* wouldn't. Using old and not especially accurate charts would be much more satisfactory.

She started to hum.

"It would take at least fourteen days to circumnavigate Tasmania —"

"I don't have that long, unfortunately."

"We could go down the east coast, or head for Citrus Island — Miss Pearmain, are you listening? I need your input to make sure you get the most out of this Experience."

Pip stopped humming and said, "I'd like to go something new — different — somewhere that other people don't always go. I live in Jellico Bay, so just seeing waves and foggy horizons isn't much of a holiday. I could see that from the beach." She looked up at him, wishing, not for the first time, for someone her own height to save her neck. Since Little Mum had gone to glory — she *did* like that term and she liked to think of Little Mum in glory — she was by far the smallest adult human she knew.

Not a little person. She had been assured of that. She didn't fit the technical or clinical description of a little person. School nurses and clinic sisters had been unreasonably interested in her progress, because she was always down at the second percentile, but eventually a sensible doctor had proclaimed what the family knew already — tiny Pippin Pearmain was exactly what one would expect from the genes handed down from the Laurels and the Pearmains.

Her only related peers were her cousins, and although they shared two of Pip's small grandparents, they had Big Nanna and Big Pop de Leon to pass them some taller genes to compensate…very much taller, in Big Nanna's case.

Knowing what she wasn't and why she was what she was gave little comfort to Pip when she must perpetually tilt her chin up to meet other people in the eye.

Maybe I can meet Jin's cousin Cèilidh. She can stand on a milking stool, and I can stand on a bucket, and we can bond over our lack of vertical stature.

Zach sighed audibly. "Miss Pearmain?"

He was in no way as sweet and appealing as young Jamie, but he seemed honest and patient. He'd have to be, to deal with small children that weren't his own, not to speak of Jin-with-a-J. Now he was dealing with Pip, and Pip was inclined to sympathise. She decided to behave. It would be kinder, and also more sensible. Misbehaving on purpose usually brought her a swat from the avenging universe.

Pip said, "Zach—Zach what?"

"Zachary Rowan."

"Another plant name. And you told me! I didn't think you would."

Actually, the name sounded a tad familiar, but she couldn't bring the context to mind. It wasn't as if she had any related children in the education system who might talk about *Mister Rowan*…or maybe *Mister Zach*.

"As I said, I'm not employed by V-S. In fact—apart from Jamie, none of us is, directly. Bart acts as an occasional provider, that's all. He didn't take this gig because it was short notice and he and his wife are marrying off their daughter."

Pip nodded, following her train of thought. "I'd like to see a bucket."

"I expect we have one somewhere. Feeling seasick?"

"I'm never sick. I just like buckets."

He looked blank.

"Interesting buckets," she pursued.

"Er—"

Probably time to stop winding the poor man up…darn it! I decided to behave.

Pip settled back and told Zachary Rowan about the bucket list with what she considered admirable coherence.

In the back of her mind, Kittisack signalled, *Tell no one,* but Jan and Lupin knew she had it, and now Lupin was gone, there was a vacancy in the circle of secrets.

Zach took it rather well.

"It's a kind of secret. Apart from me, the cats and my cousin, and now you, no living soul knows about it," Pip disclosed.

"And now I suppose you want a secret from me in exchange."

That hadn't occurred to her, but Jan and Lupin had given her secrets as an exchange for hers—one good, and one appalling.

She delved in her bag for the bucket list, turned past the page with the ellipsis and offered the green pen to Zach. "You can put it here if you want to. There is no obligation. People have a right to keep their secrets to themselves if they prefer."

Not that a—what did Jin-with-a-J call him? —a curly lad like you would have too many…

Zach gave her an odd look. "Do you mean it?"

"I'm not in the habit of telling porky pies," Pip said, channelling Magda Saxer.

Zach took the pen and wrote a few lines in a clear, modern script.

Pip took the pad back without looking at it and restored it to her messenger bag. She hoped the secret was a nice one. He deserved it to be.

Zach said, "I know of a rather interesting bucket, as it

happens. Shall I tell you some details so you can put it in your list?"

"I have to see it for it to qualify. Where is it?"

Zach said, "It's on an island, and it belongs to a special well . . .we call it Iris's Wishing Well."

Pip flashed on the Clancy bucket, but he couldn't possibly mean that unless he'd known old Clancy, which seemed unlikely. Anyway, Clancy wasn't called Iris.

"There's an exceptionally hearty lemon tree nearby," Zach said.

That *really* caught her attention, but she turned her gaze to the beautiful old chart with its fingerprint loops and whorls and fanciful drawings in the corners of the pages. She wanted to trace them with her fingertips, brailling them as she'd tried to braille the voucher before she discovered the lemon juice reveal.

That was probably a bad idea, since it might leave marks on the old paper, so she let her gaze follow the patterns instead. As she allowed her focus to soften, an odd illusion swam into her vision.

A whorl, a swirl — a whirlpool out in Bass Strait.

She blinked and it was gone. She tried to find it again.

"I want to go *here*," she said, dabbing her forefinger on the spot where the whirl had vanished.

Chapter Four. Steering

Pip expected Zach would ask whatever she meant by wanting to go somewhere without even an island, but he gave her an odd smile and said he knew the area and that it could be arranged.

"Now?" Pip asked.

"Possibly tomorrow."

"Are we going to sit here all night?"

"Certainly not. Go up on deck and have a look round. Tell Jin what you'd like for dinner."

Pip went back up the companionway and approached the rail.

She was gratified to discover they'd sailed some distance from the place she'd come aboard. Despite what Zach had said about him being qualified to sail *Tulpenmanie,* the others must be, too.

She made her way to where Jin perched in a roofed in area, apparently steering with one finger on the wheel — or was it a tiller?

"Zach said I was to tell you what I want for dinner," she said.

She thought there might be attitude with a capital A from the gem-eyed woman, but Jin nodded as if she'd expected that.

"We can do fish with salad, or a platter of figs, tomatoes, olives and brown bread, or soup and sandwiches."

"What sort of fish?" Pip enquired. The original cat and the back-up cat loved fish and so she was rather an expert.

"That depends on what we catch."

"What of the other options? Do you have to bake the bread or make the soup from scratch or land somewhere to pick tomatoes?"

"No, we have those on hand."

"The middle one, then."

Jin took a small notebook from her pocket and wrote that down. She looked up at Pip and said, "Cat-Morse?"

It could have been quid pro quo for dinner, but Pip took it as genuine curiosity. She assumed Jin would give her reply some brain-space, even if she ultimately disbelieved it.

"Cat-Morse is the way two cats I know converse with me," she explained. "Three, really, if you count Lupin's cat."

Jin said, "Who are they? Do they say anything interesting?"

"I call them the original cat and the back-up cat. I believe their real names are Kittisack and Amberjill, but my cousin Jan—that's Juniper Gin, who writes the bodice rippers—believes they're called Unseelie and Forever Autumn."

She paused to allow Jin to digest that.

Jin did so, nodded slowly and said, "I know a little queen called Mistress Calico. I wonder if she knows Cat-Morse."

"You should ask her."

"Oh, I will, although there's no guarantee she'll answer. She's the most indolent cat I've ever known. So—*do* these cats of yours say anything interesting?"

"They're not mine and they don't *say* it. I mean, they don't go *dit-dit-dah* aloud. They do Cat-Semaphore too. They communicate it, mostly with eye-blinks and tail gestures, but it gathers itself into meaning in my mind. Some of it is useful, but a lot is about manipulating me into doing what they want. Such as serving them with unreasonable amounts of cheese."

"They're cats, so that's to be expected," Jin pointed out. She gave an odd smile. "Mistress Calico has my dad wrapped right around her little white paw. It's been that way since he met her outside an exotic dance venue. She stowed away with him when he went home."

"Your dad goes to exotic dance venues. What does your mum think?"

"Oh, she goes with him. She's an exotic dancer, so it would be odd if she didn't."

"I dance too," Pip confided.

"Exotically?"

"Not so far, unless you count fan dancing. I learned ballet for a role when I was younger."

"Oh?"

"Yes. I played a child dancer in a series called *En Pointe*. It was based on a trilogy of ballet stories from the late fifties, and they had a real retired ballet principal as technical adviser. I don't think they took a lot of notice of her, though. I can remember her getting very cross with the director when he wanted us taught quite advanced stuff that she said was incorrect in context."

"And you played the starriest of star child roles?" Jisinia sounded a wee bit mocking.

Pip shook her head. "Of course not. That was down to one of the cast who'd been dancing since she could walk. I didn't even start until I was eight. I liked it, though, and I've kept up my practice ever since. I do it at seven every weekday morning."

"That might be awkward on a yacht."

"Not a bit," Pip said. She tapped her phone which was wedged into the side pocket of her messenger bag. "I have music in here."

"Sugar Plum? Swan Lake?"

"No, mostly Drozdov, and a few pieces by Ness Mac-Connel at present. I mix it up. Mostly it's basic exercises, but I do free dancing, too."

"It was Drozdov you were doing on the sand," Jin said.

"That's right. It seemed appropriate."

Jin nodded. Then she snapped her gaze onto Pip and said abruptly, "Do you have a cat in your mind?"

Pip put dance practice out of her thoughts. "What an odd idea. I don't. I'm human. I'm not so sure of the cats, though."

"Whether they're human?" Jin sounded as if she was taking it quite seriously, but apart from the annoying Trip, Pip had found the people involved with Vouch-Safe unexpectedly easy to talk to. That was unusual, as other than her family and Sully, she had seldom found anyone she liked to be with for long. There had been little Angie Blake and her mum, and more recently old Mister Clancy, but most people operated on a wavelength a long way from hers. Trying to stay relevant to their conversation made her tired.

She started to hum, contemplating the various groups of people she'd not blended in with over her six decades.

She'd had hotbed friendships, but most of that had been on the side of the older actors who had adopted her as a mascot.

Probably I should have been friends with other performers, but they've almost never been the same kind of performer as I am.

She remembered just one who *had* been on her wavelength... He was the only one she had actively looked forward to working with again. It had never happened.

"Miss Pearmain? Are you implying your cats might be human?" Jin sounded as if she had asked a variation of that before.

"Obviously not."

"You said you weren't sure of them."

Pip sent her mind back over the conversation before she'd wandered off into the memory of badly fitting acquaintances and one who might have fitted very well if circumstances had been different. "Oh, I see. I meant I wasn't sure if they were really cats. Ordinary cats. Unless all cats use Cat-Morse and no one has happened to mention it to me?"

"None of the ones I know use it," Jin said.

"Do you know a lot of cats?"

"Quite a few. I know Mistress Calico best, and one called Magpie pretty well. Mind you, he's getting along in years. There are others, too. I say none of them use Cat-Morse, but since I didn't know it was a thing, it might be more accurate to say I don't have enough information. Pity Bart and Brigitta don't keep a ship's cat on *Mad Tulip*, because if they did, we could have spent your Experience experimenting. Most remiss of them."

"Do yachts have ship's cats?"

"Obviously, they ought to." She frowned. "Now, what were we discussing before we got on to cats and Cat-Morse, Miss Pearmain?"

"Dinner," Pip said readily. "What I wanted."

"That's it. Do you want to steer *Mad Tulip* while I go and see to conjuring up some food?"

"Is that legal?"

"What — conjuring food?"

"Leaving a novice to steer a yacht."

Jin shrugged. "How would I know? I've been sharing a bed with the temporary skipper for quite a while, but he's never said anything about legality. If it helps, we're well clear of the shipping lanes and I set a few wards. *Mad Tulip* knows where she's going and there's nothing to trouble us here, unless we bounce off a whale, and that really isn't likely."

Pip was going to accept the offer, but Zach loomed up before she could do so. "Jin, what did I tell you—"

"Miss Pearmain would like to steer the ship," Jin said blandly.

"Then she may," Zach said. He pulled up a low chair and sat close by the wheel—unless it was a tiller. "Okay, Miss Pearmain, steer away...but I'll take over if we see another vessel."

"Or a whale," Pip said.

"That's not likely unless we run into migrating Antarctic blues."

"Better not do that," Jin said.

"Not literally! I just meant we might see them, though it's getting a bit late in the season."

Jin slithered out of the captain's chair and vanished towards the galley.

Pip took her place. She wondered if she ought to ask for a cushion to raise herself, but Zach indicated a pedal that lifted the chair beautifully.

A much, much nicer version of a dentist's chair.

Pip settled down to steer the yacht.

CHAPTER FIVE. THE THIRD CREWMAN

The sun had set spectacularly by the time dinner was served. Pip chose to eat it on deck.

By then, Zach was steering, and Jin, who had been annoying him for the last half hour, had disappeared again to apply herself to laying out the meal, which she brought up from the galley.

"Do you have camomile tea?" Pip asked without much hope. She supposed she ought to have brought a supply with her. She'd probably have to settle for cambric tea instead.

Zach said, "That can be arranged. I'm sure Brigitta has some, along with some revolting stuff she refers to as *Geistbohne.*"

Brigitta, Pip recalled, was one of the people who owned the yacht. "She's not here, though."

"That doesn't mean her tea can't be," Jin said. She vanished to the galley yet again and presently brought up a mugful of fragrant tea for Pip and a belligerently powerful coffee brew for Zach.

He gave her what Pip recalled was referred to as *an old-fashioned look.* "I won't be drinking that, Mistress Jisinia."

"I will then." She somehow produced a more moderate drink for him and ostentatiously sipped the steaming black horror herself.

Pip saw her eyes widen.

Turning her attention to her own drink, she saw the mug was printed with the yacht's name, and that it featured a bunch of rainbow mixed tulips. "Does *Tulpenmanie* really have something to do with tulips?" she asked, examining the painted blooms. They were certainly not the sort one bought in pack of six mixed bulbs from the small Jellico Bay nursery. They reminded her of Little Mum's desire for novelty.

Zach said evenly, "Yes — it means *tulip madness, or tulip mania.*"

Hence *Mad Tulip*, Pip thought.

"It's Dutch, then. After the inflation that hit tulip bulbs in the Netherlands?"

"Yes, that's right." Zach added, "Bart's mother is Dutch, and she runs a tulip farm over at West Cape."

"I know it. *Marieke's Kleine Nederlanden.* My mother used to get catalogues from there." She reflected sadly on the dozens of catalogues Little Mum had collected and kept for the outstanding photographs. Each catalogue was a work of art. Thirty years' worth of them were stored in boxes, having never been unpacked since her move from Delmsford. Maybe that last order, forever unfulfilled, lurked among them.

Little Mum had wanted to plant firebird tulips, which she'd never seen or heard of before they appeared in the catalogue.

Futility swept over Pip. Little Mum's life had not been exciting, but the things that made her happy shouldn't be kept in the dark.

I'll get those catalogues out and maybe make collages. Jan might like some. Or, I could offer them back to the tulip place for a display. Maybe they could go in decoupage.

She had only the vaguest notion of what that was…something with pictures stuck to boxes or vases and varnished into place, perhaps? Maybe it was something to investigate when she got home.

After all, if Jan and Lupin can go off making pottery, maybe I could try decoupage with bits of catalogue. I'd need a vase or a box…no, a bucket! *I could have a decoupage bucket and then I'd have a new one to add to my bucket list. Easy-peasy.*

She shrugged off melancholy. Decoupaging a bucket might be an adventure in itself.

Wonder if Jan would like to have a go. She has been trying new things.

Taking her tea with her, she walked a little unsteadily to the stern of the yacht, where she watched the wake, sipped tea, and ate a Strawberry Fool on the Hill tart which Jin had unexpectedly produced for dessert.

She wondered where Jin shopped for those tarts. Did she have a local patisserie that stocked them, or was she a mail-order customer?

Ask her.

She asked.

Jin said, vaguely, "I have an arrangement with someone who gets them in."

"Into Tasmania? I get mine from Jelly-and-Juice."

"I live in Victoria, mostly."

"Ja. *Und?*"

Jin said, "As I said, I have an arrangement. A lot of us have."

"Us?"

"Us. Miss Pearmain, has anyone ever suggested you can be annoyingly persistent?"

"Frequently," Pip said. "Why won't you tell me? I told you."

"Because you already have your source. I have my source. We don't need one another's."

"Unless you're in Tasmania."

Jin threw up her hands and flounced away.

Pip smiled to herself. Winding up Jisinia was fun.

The breeze had dropped.

She wondered how Jamie was faring with the cats and her cottage.

Maybe I should have put the cats' food in the sink instead of the fridge. It might still be a bit frozen.

"Zach!" she called, over her shoulder.

"Miss Pearmain?" He came up alongside her and leaned over the stern rail. Goodness knew who was steering with Jisinia off in a flounce and Zach away from the wheel . . .unless it was a tiller.

Better not ask.

"Do you have a phone number for Jamie?"

"I have one, but we're not supposed to hand them out."

Pip frowned. "What do you think I'm going to do with it? Harass him with inappropriate texts? Hack his Catch Me Here page? Breathe at him until he gets a shiver down his back? I just want to let him know where the cats' food is that needs taking out of the fridge."

Zach extracted his own mobile from his shirt pocket and tapped it awake. He hit a saved number and waited for it to pick up.

"Jamie, I have Miss Pearmain on the line regarding her cats' food."

Pip took the phone. "On the line indeed. That makes me sound like a fish. Are the cats behaving?"

"More or less," Jamie's voice said cautiously.

That probably meant they weren't.

"If you bribe them with cheese it will be easier. They're anyone's for cheese. Have you had any trouble with the lemon tree?"

"Not a lot."

That meant he had.

Shouldn't have mentioned it. If I hadn't he might not have gone to look. Reverse psychology.

"Your dog isn't peeing on my camomile, I hope."

"I told you he wouldn't, and he hasn't."

"Is he bothering the cats?"

"No."

"Are the cats bothering him?"

"No. They seem to quite like him."

"Good. If two magpies turn up in the morning, they're called Two and Joy and they'll demand cheese. They can have a wee bit. Too much isn't good for them. Don't give them bacon, though. It's not good for them *at all*. Oh, and—"

Zach gently removed the phone from Pip's palm. "Over and out," he said, and switched it off.

"Hey!" Pip glowered at him.

"Miss Pearmain, this Experience is about *new* things—not staying at home in your head."

"But I didn't get to tell him where the cat food is!"

"He'll work it out. He's an eighteen-year-old lad. Boys that age *always* work out food. It's in their DNA."

Pip was still annoyed, but she persuaded herself to relax. Zach was probably right, in a way. She should be enjoying her Experience. The cats had seemed positively to want her out of the house.

Eh – why? What are they up to? Do they really like that dog, or are they lulling it so they can attack its tail while it's blamelessly asleep?

"Where do we sleep?" she asked, dragging herself away from the possibly hair-raising activities of Kittisack and Amberjill. She absolved Lupin's cat from any possible feline plot. What could a wonky model cat with beautiful decorations orchestrate in the way of mayhem?

It had been a full day, and by now she was almost as tired as she'd been on the day of the Delmsford Flower Show.

For the first time since Magda Saxer's call, Pip wondered if she could still negotiate the early morning calls, long hours of makeup and costume, bad coffee, and multiple long days of filming with people she didn't know.

It had been a while since she was last in that Petri dish.

Sully won't be there to keep my edges and corners in check. How am I going to manage?

"There's a cabin you can use if you like privacy, or you can bunk down in the chartroom with the rest of us if you prefer the full crew experience," Zach said, breaking in on her un-comfortable doubts.

"I expect I'll do that. I always sleep alone—aside from the cats—so it might be novel to share a room. I don't take up much space."

She might have left it there, but something occurred to her. "Where's the other one? The third crewman? Jamie said there was another person—his uncle—on board."

CHAPTER SIX. TRIPLE ZERO

The question seemed to take Zach by surprise. "Ah…"

Pip's *B-S-on-the-horizon* meter clicked in. She could almost always tell when someone was prevaricating.

Just like Little Nanna Laurel.

After all, she was pretty good at it herself. She hardly ever told a direct fib, but she implied, evaded and eluded like a champion.

She pushed Zach for information. "I know he was here—I saw him from the beach, helping you lower the dinghy. Where's he gone?"

"Maybe he went for a swim," Zach said unconvincingly.

"Is that safe? What about the whales?"

They hadn't seen any whales, but the idea of anyone swimming in the unpredictable waters of Bass Strait in the semi-darkness for what must be several hours by now seemed suicidal.

Boats disappeared at sea. People sometimes vanished from cruise ships. Something along those lines hooked at her memory.

Barnabas Singer vanished from a boat while his mate was scuba diving back in 1999. That was one of those search and rescue stories. He was supposed to be invigilating for his mate. Instead, he was the one who went missing.

She frowned, trying to recall the aftermath. She had a feeling he'd turned up later, somewhere else, with no plausible explanation for his absence, but she couldn't remember the details.

Trudy Riley and Debra Finnigan went exploring with their canoe around Hypatia Island and disappeared in 1922. There were grainy pictures of them with their nineteen twenties shingles and their long beads.

Pip remembered the short *Australia Unexplained* film segment made for the fiftieth anniversary of the girls' disappearance. They'd started with a scene with the girls riding their bikes and another of them at a dance, establishing them as active young women with a lively social life before switching to the trip to Hypatia Island in a boating expedition with friends and family.

Pip had acted the part of one of Debra's sisters at the island picnic in the dramatisation. The other sister was played by the real Debra's great-niece—Melissa Finnigan. Goodness! That was fifty years ago. Where was Melissa now? Maybe the surviving actors could reconvene for a centenary re-make.

Must tell Sully.

No—

Must tell Magda.

There had been other disappearances, but these weren't the one Pip half remembered—not the one triggering her apprehension. That one was a much more recent event, surely no more than four or five years ago.

"It's probably not safe for you to go swimming at night, certainly not for me, and possibly not for Jin—but Tane is half fish, so he'll be fine." Zach was probably trying to sound soothing, but to Pip his tone struck a false note.

"He's a merman?" she asked sarcastically. It seemed a lot less likely than her half-formulated theory that Jin's cousin Cèilidh might be a witch. Indeed, that seemed ridiculous to her now.

Tiny Pippin Pearmain, fey and flighty and childlike...

That's not really me. Not the whole me. Not always me.

Zach didn't answer.

"Whatever he is, he'd better not be drowning out there."

Pip frowned and strove to speak in a clear and reasonable tone. "I mean that, Zach. People swim the English Channel, but no one would be daft enough to swim in Bass Strait at night. Not this far from the shore. And if he's scuba diving, he's been down far too long."

She felt her heartbeat rising.

She was on a yacht out in the strait with two strangers who might have disposed of a third. No one knew she was there...except for Jamie and possibly the annoying Trip.

I ought to have let Jan know—or Magda Saxer, even. I should have texted them.

Mystery tours indeed. How do I even know this was Lupin's idea?

A calming thought struck her.

Could this be part of the Experience? Something like a murder mystery weekend, only with a disappearance? Could the uncle be First Victim, and I'm supposed to investigate?

She remembered the little pantomime Lupin and Jan had staged for her benefit, back at the flower show.

And I knew them. I should have known they were playacting.

That was a better idea, but even so...

No. For that scenario to work I'd need to have been introduced to him before he vanished. There's no emotional investment when someone disappears, and I have no idea what sort of person he is. Emotional investment is as important to Experiences as it is to plays and films. Besides, we'd need a bigger cast.

She dug in the side of her messenger bag for her phone.

Zach looked uneasy. "Miss Pearmain, who are you calling?"

"Triple zero. Obviously."

"Don't do that. Please."

Well, he wouldn't want that if it is a murder weekend thingie...oh, but then he'd laugh and 'fess up, and show me a brochure or something. Or he could show me Jamie's uncle's certificate for record-breaking dives... is four hours really too long?

She had no real knowledge of the hours, depths, or oxygen tank algorithms.

After all, she didn't dive.

Zach looked harried.

Pip backed away from the rail. A pleasantly bizarre conversation with a friendly young man had morphed into something scary with astonishing speed.

She had no idea if there was danger to her or not, but there *had* been a third crewman. She'd seen him. Jamie had referred to him as his uncle. He'd said everyone loved him, but that he was *different*.

Zach had also mentioned him. He'd suggested there was a volatile relationship between Jamie's uncle and Jin and in retrospect that seemed sinister.

Surely not some kind of mad love triangle with added murder . . .or a side of suicide.

"What's going on?" Jin had come up behind her and put a hand on Pip's shoulder to avoid a collision.

Pip flinched and dipped her shoulder out of the way.

Zach said, in a harassed tone, "Miss Pearmain is asking about Tane."

Jin moved to stand by her boyfriend's side, presenting a united pair against Pip's single outsider. "What about Tane?" Her bi-coloured eyes looked wary in the light streaming from the wheelhouse, but she sounded puzzled rather than apprehensive.

Pip said, "Jamie told me his uncle was aboard — and Zach said that where you and he were concerned *all bets are off*."

"So? I'm bloody annoying. Ants-in-the-jam annoying. Tane's even more bloody annoying — just this side of wasps-at-a-picnic annoying. Right, Zach?"

Zach half-smiled and nodded. "I can attest to that." He put his arm around Jin.

"Therefore, we have the odd brangle," Jin said. "We'd be disappointed if we didn't. In fact, we had one earlier."

"I saw him helping with the dinghy, but he wasn't here when I came aboard."

"He was though…remember Zach called for the winch? Tane was in charge of that."

"Then where is he now? Call him. Introduce us."

Jin shrugged with feline grace. "Not much point calling. I expect he's gone overboard."

"Jin…" Zach sounded exasperated.

Jin turned her head to look at him. Since she was tall, she could do that without tilting her chin. "What's got your knickers in a knot, Zach?"

Pip backed up a few more steps.

"She doesn't mean *gone overboard* the way it sounds," Zach said, reaching out a conciliatory hand as if he could bridge some gap in their mutual understanding.

"Doesn't she? What other way could it be? Explain that to me."

"Well—"

"Don't start with *well*," Pip said irritably. She lowered her finger to the zero on her phone. A faint tone sounded.

"Miss Pearmain, please don't do that!"

"Explain." Pip depressed the zero again.

At the back of her mind, this felt like a scene from a melodrama.

"Tane is *fine*," Jin put in with a burst of impatience.

"Then where is he?"

"I told you, he went overboard," Jin said. "He was going on and on and *on*—"

Pip pressed the final zero and flicked the phone to speaker, to prove she'd done as she proclaimed.

You have dialled emergency Triple Zero. Your call is being connected.

Pip hadn't expected this. Was the thing going to invite her to leave a message?

She tried to compose one on the fly.

Help! I'm stuck on a yacht called Tulpenmanie out in Bass Strait with two people who say the third crewman has gone overboard, only —

"Great bogle!" Jin snapped. She made a snatching motion, and suddenly Pip's phone was in her hand.

CHAPTER SEVEN. INTERVIEW IN HER HEAD

Pip opened her mouth to yell *Fire*. She'd heard that was the most effective way to summon help. Most people automatically paid attention if one yelled *Fire*.

The futility of yelling *Fire* in the middle of the strait was the only thing that stopped her. Even if help heard her, it would be too late for the missing crewman and probably for her by the time it arrived.

She imagined herself wrapped in a thermal blanket and being plied with hot sweet tea while a sympathetic police officer told her to *take your time* . . .

She'd report the missing man with clarity and aplomb and tell the story multiple times to multiple people, and it would sound more and more unlikely with each repetition.

They'd have her second-guessing her memories in no time. They probably wouldn't believe her.

She played the probable interview in her head.

"You say you didn't actually meet this individual, Ms Pearmain?"

"Miss. I'm not *mis*erable."

"You didn't actually meet this individual you say is missing?"

"No, but I know his name. Tane. He's Jamie's uncle."

"Jamie is—"

"The V-S driver. I told you that before."

"I don't seem to have that in my notes."

Maybe I told the last person that.

"Do you have a contact number for Jamie?"

"No. No one would give me one."

"What is his surname?"

"He wouldn't tell me that, either. I just know he's eighteen and has a sister called Laura. He's staying at my cottage at six Ribston Lane, Jellico Bay. The property is called *Lemonwood.*"

The interviewer *du jour* would *look* at her. What sixty-something woman let a stranger whose full name she didn't know stay at her house while she was away? Especially someone of an age to have rowdy parties and drop pizza down the back of the couch.

Her credibility would drop another notch, as if her age, sex and size were not enough... And let's not forget the occupation, or lack of one, she thought sourly. *Washed up B actor...or was she a C actor? Trying to get attention.*

"Ms Pearmain, are you sure this missing person was ever aboard? That's right, you saw them. Can you give a detailed description?"

She sought in her memory, but it had been just a vague impression of someone tall, shaggy-haired and shirtless, and wearing...a kilt? A sulu? A lavalava? Maybe a towel wrapped around his middle? Definitely, it had been a *he.*

Aside from a cheeky mental *Oo-la-la* at the lack of shirt — Pip had always been partial to male chests — she hadn't taken much notice, being more focused on Zach as he approached in the dinghy. When they reached the yacht, Jin had dropped the rope ladder, and Pip had climbed up, to converse with Jin while Zach arrived and — yes! — called out for someone to operate the winch.

Then what? Jin fetched the green PFD and in the novelty of being aboard *Tulpenmanie* Pip had utterly forgotten the third crewman.

Tulpenmanie has a multicoloured sail. Surely, a murderous

couple wouldn't be quite so gratuitously noticeable! Or discuss Cat-Morse. Or ask if I had a cat in my head. Or call me Miss Pearmain without constant reminding that I am female, single, and not miserable. Or give me my favourite tea and a beautiful tart for dessert.

A voice—human this time—asked which service she required. Pip heard because the phone was still on speaker.

"Jin." Zach's voice sounded calm.

Jin blinked. "Oh. Yes." She detached from her boyfriend's arm and closed the space between herself and Pip, holding Pip's phone out on her palm like an offering.

She smelled of wintersweet, a nostalgic scent that took Pip suddenly back to Little Mum's garden at *Treasures*.

Surely no one who smelled of wintersweet could be evilly intended.

Pip flinched but reached out tentatively and took the phone.

"I'm sorry for that," Jin said softly.

"For what? Winding me up or stealing my phone?"

"Both. Everything. Ants-in-the-jam. I'm too impulsive but I'm trying to do better." Jin cast a betraying glance at Zach. "So I'm sorry and I'll do my best not to do any of it again."

"Do what you need to, Miss Pearmain," Zach said from over by the rail.

Jin returned to lean beside him.

The voice on the phone repeated the request for information for what must have been the fourth or fifth time.

Pip looked down at the screen and assumed an upbeat, spry and elderly manner. "I'm sorry—I'm okay. One of the grandkids got hold of my phone and I've just got it back. They watch too much telly. I apologise for the trouble."

"You are saying you don't need assistance?"

"I am saying I don't need assistance. I'll delete this call log, so I don't accidently pocket-dial you." She achieved a light laugh. "That's the term, isn't it?"

"Have a good day," the voice said.

They must hear all sorts of excuses...

She deleted the log and slid the phone back into her bag. Then she stared across at Zach and Jin.

"One of the *grandkids*?" Jin said, lifting the eyebrow over her green eye. The one over her blue eye stayed absolutely level.

"I assume you're someone's grandkid. I am a grandkid, though my grandparents aren't around anymore. Everyone is *someone*'s grandkid," Pip excused herself.

"Not yours, though."

"Not a chance. Even if I had any children, which I don't, I'm sure the dates wouldn't quite work. How old are you?"

"Twenty-nine."

Pip nodded sagely. She'd been right. It would have been possible, but not particularly likely for her to have had a grandchild of Jisinia's age.

She went on contemplating the odd young woman. Jin was an even odder young woman than she'd initially thought.

I wouldn't have minded having her as a grandchild, actually.

Jin was nothing like darling Angie, who had danced through Pip's life back in the day, but she had class. She was *trying* to do better. She admitted her faults, but that was worth nothing without the earnest intention to do better. Jisinia had expressed that intention.

"Why did you not follow through with the call?" Zach asked.

"Why did you make Jin give my phone back?" Pip countered.

Zach laughed. "Excuse me, but the idea of me making Jin do anything is hilarious."

"I thought she was your girlfriend."

Oops. My age is showing.

"I mean, I thought she would want to please you — and that you would equally want to please her."

"I *say* she's my girlfriend. It's more that I'm her plaything." His voice was even, but Pip detected an undertone of truth. "But never mind that now," he said.

Pip remembered the savage cup of coffee and thought Zach was possibly deluding himself. He'd had the backbone to refuse it.

She turned her attention to the woman again. "How did you get your hands on my phone, Jisinia?"

"I grabbed it," Jin said glibly.

"From way over there?"

"I'm fast on my feet."

"She is that," Zach said, nodding.

"Enabler," Pip said to Zach. She switched her gaze to Jin. "Enabled."

They stared at her.

Maybe those weren't the right terms.

Pip gave up on that. After all, Jin had given the phone back with the call still in play. She returned to the original point. "Where is Jamie's uncle?"

Jin said, "He really went overboard, as I said. He's fine. It was his idea. He's at home in the water, just as much as he is on land. You can ask him what happened when he comes back."

"If he comes back," Zach said. He added hastily, "Not because he's drowned or anything—"

"You can't possibly drown Tane," Jin put in.

"—just that he might have found something better to do."

"Or some*one*. Probably Jillian Jules," Jin said.

Pip gazed at them with displeasure. "You two ought to be on the stage. Are you going to explain this to me, or not?"

"I think we'll leave it up to Tane," Jin said.

Pip thought wistfully of Lemonwood Cottage, the original cat, the back-up cat, Lupin's cat, and the camomile tea she'd be consuming right now before retiring to her single bed.

"Might I have another cup of tea?" she asked.
Jin went off to make it.

Chapter Eight. The Heaven and Earth Ring

Pip went to lean on the rail beside Zach who, according to nice young Jamie, was the user-friendly option.

"Are you really a schoolteacher?"

"I am."

"Then why are you here?" She waved her hand around *Tulpenmanie*.

"Long holidays leave me with time on hand. My stepdad taught Nik—my stepbrother—and me to sail when we were in our teens. Nik turned into a proper yachtie and dock-hound, and a few years back when his daughter was taking up his attention he asked if I wanted some work at the marina—hence I started crewing on *Tulpenmanie*," Zach said. "I got along well with the skipper, and now I sometimes sub for him when he has somewhere else to be."

"Is that it?"

"I used to do some other crew work, but now I spend a fair bit of time with Jin, so I don't bother." He gave her a sideways smile. "I quite enjoy being Jin's plaything, by the way. It's interesting. Entertaining."

"So, what is she?"

Zach's smile turned into a surprised stare.

Pip made an impatient gesture. "Is she a teacher too?"

Zach shook his head.

"She crews for boats?"

"Sometimes. Mostly on *Tulpenmanie*, because she likes

annoying me."

"As in—"

"She has some interesting talents that mean she can do some things faster and more efficiently than I can, or even Bart."

"And Tane—who can't be drowned. What does *he* do when he's not manning winches or going overboard?"

"Oh, he's a jeweller—a silversmith. He goes around the markets with his dad, who's also a silversmith. Their cousin's husband often goes along to keep them in check. Tane's inclined to be a bit O-T-T, and his dad...life of the party. They're all fun to be around, and Merry and Tane make quality jewellery. They do repairs-while-you-wait, too."

"Brilliant!"

"What's brilliant in that?" Zach asked cautiously.

Pip opened her messenger bag and took Sully's tektite ring out of its soft pouch. She huffed on it and gave it a vigorous polish. "I can ask him to have a look at this."

Zach squinted at it. "It doesn't look like one of Tane's or his dad's."

"It wouldn't be. My agent gave it to me back when I was seven. She called it a *heaven and earth* ring." She poked it with a spare finger. "It's vintage—if not antique. I've had it for nearly sixty years, and goodness knows where or when Sully got it. I never thought to ask her, and now it's too late."

"Tane is nowhere near sixty and he's not a gem historian." Zach seemed to be trying to keep up.

"That doesn't matter. He might be able to tell me something about this—its provenance—but what I really want to ask him is if it can be altered to fit me."

"You've had a ring for nearly sixty years, and it doesn't fit? Did it ever?"

"No. I don't know if you've noticed, but I have small hands."

"They match the rest of you."

"Yes, but Sully had big hands. She was a big woman, like Big Nanna de Leon. When I was young, I kept thinking eventually I'd get big enough to wear it, but now I have to admit that *probably* isn't going to happen..."

Zach looked confused. "Isn't the term *certainly*?"

"It would be, but there was one person who was a lot shorter than average but who was classed as a giant when he died... but I think he had a medical condition that made him grow...a pituitary tumour, or something."

If anything, Zach's confusion grew. "You have a—"

"No! I'm as fit as a flea. I can't even remember this person's name. Never met him. I just read about him somewhere." Pip sighed, and went on, "Once I took my ring to be resized and the jeweller said it was gimcrack and wouldn't do it. He wanted to sell me another one—he said it would be a better investment than paying for my ring to be fixed. He implied tektites had no intrinsic value."

"Only investment and intrinsic value isn't the point," Zach said.

"No. So I told him. I doubt if he'll patronise a little old lady again after what I said to him." She raised her brows. "Why *do* people think they can patronise little old ladies? Any ladies? Or little *young* ladies, come to that?"

"I wouldn't know. Maybe it's unconscious. If you catch me patronising you, feel free to complain."

"I will. Or maybe I'll turn you over to Jisinia to be disciplined." She paused to let that sink in. "Speaking of rings, you and Jin aren't engaged?" She'd noted the lack of jewellery on Jin's beautiful hands, although she wore a crystal on a chain around her neck.

"We're not."

"Why not?"

"We're just—not. The question has not been asked. An

offer has never been made, or even suggested."

"Fair enough. I'm not engaged either. Never was."

Zach said, "You can show the ring to Tane when he comes back, but I can't guarantee he'll be able to do anything. I can guarantee he won't make a stupid remark or patronise you. He might proposition you, but you can always say *no*."

"Whyever would he do that?"

Zach pulled a small face. "Tane propositions almost everyone. It's in his DNA."

"You?"

"Of course, me. I said *no thank you*, so he laughed and offered me a cup of cider instead."

"Why?"

"I like cider. Oh, you mean why did I refuse – that's because I'm straight."

"Scared, you mean." Jin had returned with the camomile tea for Pip and more moderate coffee for herself and Zach. She looked curiously at the ring in Pip's palm. "Ooh, I like that. It swallows the light and gives it back in the silver."

"I like it too," Pip said.

She had a rare impulse to give the ring to Jin, just as she'd once had the impulse to give *Grandmother's Sunshine* to Angie Blake, but she held it back. If anyone gave Jin a ring it ought to be Zach. If the heaven and earth ring went to anyone but Pip, it ought to be to Jan's daughter, Clarkia, or else to a child performer who needed a bit of luck.

Pip dropped it back into the pouch and out of temptation before accepting the tea.

"What do you mean, scared? What is there to be scared of in being propositioned? As Zach said, you can always say no."

Jin sighed. "It was a silly quip. I *am* trying to stop doing that. The thing with Tane is that he's annoying but – " She did her feline shrug. "There is no need for *anyone* to be scared of him. I'm sure he's lovely in bed. Or in the water. Or swinging from the porch roof. And I don't know that from personal experience. I've known Tane all my life. My dad has friends at the falls, so my brother and I used to swim with the kids there. Tane was one of the shepherds who made sure the falls kids remembered Corin's and my limitations."

Pip nodded, seeing what Jin probably meant.

Children who grew up near swimming holes might easily forget visiting inland children might not be as at home in the water as they were.

"That puts me, and Corin, in one of the rare categories that Tane doesn't proposition. Sort of uncle-to-niece or nevvie. It's like Zach and aunts."

"Zach doesn't proposition aunts?"

Jisinia laughed. "Zach doesn't proposition anyone, much. It's the other way round. Aunts love him. When I first met him he made sure I wasn't an aunt."

"I'm not an aunt," Pip said sadly. "But what's wrong with them? I had an aunt. Little Mum's sister."

"It's to do with his job," Jisinia said, since Zach seemed disinclined to comment. "Early childhood teacher. That means he's forever running into yummy mummies and eager aunts. The kids love Mister Zach, and it seems to be catching. That's all."

Zach said, "It's nowhere near as bad as Jisinia makes it sound. She's fanaticising."

"I used to teach dancing at a playgroup," Pip said, remembering. "It was great fun. I didn't have any trouble with aunts."

"I should think not," Jisinia said, grinning. "Any predatory aunt would run for her life if you gave her a *look*."

Pip sipped her tea sleepily. It was camomile, all right, but it had an extra gentle sweetness in it, as if it had flowered under a kinder sun.

The adrenaline burst from her near brush with triple zero had left her feeling drained, but the tea, and the silly conversation regarding aunts and silversmiths worked their soothing magic.

Zach and Jin hadn't explained anything properly, but she absolved them of murdering their crewmate. Now she came to think of it, she had noticed the threesome having what Jin referred to as a *bit of a brangle* when launching the dinghy. Presumably Tane had used the winch and abandoned ship immediately afterwards while still comfortably in sight of land. He might even have caught a lift with Jamie—what could be more natural than to go off with his nephew? He might even now be schmoozing with Kittisack and Amberjill while Jamie's dog communed with Lupin's cat.

That left the puzzle of how Jin and Zach thought Tane would re-join them now they were well away from the coast, but Pip was confident she would think of a feasible method— if only she wasn't so tired. She was always good at plotting.

She finished her tea and handed the cup to Jin. "Is it okay if I turn in now?"

"I'll show you the bathroom—it's just off the chartroom," Jin said.

Pip thought she should have been shown that before, but then—she'd forgotten to show Jan the one at Lemonwood.

"I can manage," she said. "I'll sleep in the chartroom—unless you two would prefer to have it to yourselves?"

The couple exchanged speculative glances and Zach said, "We'll be fine," which might mean anything.

Maybe they don't sleep together that way. Maybe they're the new chaste. Is that a real term, or did I just make it up? What would I know?

Chapter Nine. Remembering Alain and Varian

"I'll switch the light on for you," Jin said.

She didn't move, but as Pip headed down the companion-way, the chartroom lit up.

Must be a remote switch. Maybe a time delay, so I'd better hurry.

Pip perceived a rather odd swag tucked into a corner. It hadn't been there before. It had a paper with her name on it pinned to the top end, so she went to the bathroom—or was that called *the head* on a yacht?—and cleaned up. She'd forgotten a nightgown in her rapid packing, but she had the over-length T-shirt in her messenger bag. That would do. It covered her decently to her knees, and if Jin and Zach couldn't bear the accidental glimpse of middle-aged calves as she shuffled off to the loo at 3 a.m., then they had led much more sheltered lives than seemed probable.

Younger people *should* see middle-aged bodies as a normal thing, she thought. It lets them know there's nothing to fear. Change is just change.

Mind you…my middle-aged body is in better shape than most.

After that smug thought, she almost heard Kittisack give a nasty Cat-Morse snigger and hastily amended it to *but then, I have fortunate genes, I've never had children, I've led a well-nour-ished life, and my ballet practice keeps me toned.*

You're still being smug, the mental Kittisack commented. *You feel virtuous when you think of that ballet practice.*

Pip sighed and resolved to wear without complaint whatever little chastisement the universe decided to dish out. She assumed there would be a reckoning. In her experience, smugness, along with deliberate bad behaviour, almost never went unpunished.

She wiggled down into the swag, concertinaing and jack-knifing to make sure there was adequate room. The base rustled slightly as if it was stuffed with hay or dry leaves, and it smelled heavenly…somewhat like a mix of autumn leaves and dry salt air.

The upper part was state-of-the-art modern with toggles. Pip frowned as she nestled in. She wondered what the cats were up to and whether they'd joined Jamie in his bed.

His own bed. How peculiar of him to supply his own bed to…what did he say? To curl up in.

I bet those cats are Cat-Morsing for all they're worth and he's…well, doing whatever young men do in beds. Maybe he's still in the kitchen, drinking my camomile tea with his uncle.

Her thoughts shifted.

Is toggles what I mean? Units of warmth…or are they the thingies they used to fasten cloaks in The House of Heriot?

She smiled, remembering her role in that 1970s flick. She'd been sixteen—but had looked no more than twelve—when her character, Marigold Heriot, had been stolen away by a highwayman on a horse in the dead of night. They'd wanted to use a stuntwoman for that part, but Pip and Sully had argued for Pip to do it. Alain Barfleur, who'd played the highwayman, had laughed and said, *why not?* He guaranteed tiny Pippin Pearmain would be utterly safe with him and his horse, Varian.

Gorgeous beastie…so calm in the stable, but bright and shining as the sky when the cameras rolled… Maybe if I'd known he wasn't always so calm I wouldn't have wanted to do it…

But Pip knew she would.

She'd never been brave, but Alain had been a dashing young man, then. He'd had fair hair and grey eyes, and he'd always smelled faintly of fresh toast. That seemed an odd scent for a man to choose, even in the hippy-trippy days of long hair and unisex bell bottoms and ponchos, but she'd been too shy to ask about it. She'd been a wee bit smitten with him. Maybe he'd noticed, but he'd been kind and brotherly to her. Possibly, he genuinely thought she was a little kid. Or could be Sully had had *a word*. Sully was famed for her *words*.

They'd had fun, ranging around the extensive grounds of Oakengrove, walking along the beach, and riding double on Varian.

That had been *after* the abduction scene, but as Alain said, you never knew when the director might want a retake, or even a new scene.

He'd been right to consider that. Having observed them down by the sea on a rest day, the director, whose name Pip couldn't remember, had decided a moonlit beach scene would add to the story arc of the highwayman's redemption.

"Why moonlight?" Sully had demanded, no doubt totting up the risks to her young client.

Pip herself had answered that one. "The highwayman couldn't ride around the village in daylight. Someone might see him and report him to...to..." Her inventiveness was fine, but her lack of knowledge of local law enforcement in the early nineteenth century was shaky. "What word do I want?" she'd asked Alain.

"I don't know, Pipkin. We don't have things like that where I come from."

"Things like what? Policemen?"

"No need for them," he'd said.

"Hippy."

"I *beg* your pardon?"

"Never mind. The highwayman couldn't ride round in the day, anyway."

He'd laughed at that.

The moonlit ride, during which he'd dismounted and lifted

Pip-as-Marigold down to walk beside him had been fun, even when Varian, usually so impeccably mannered, decided to paw up some wet, salty sand and shower his master and Pip with it.

That had been a good time. Alain had given Pip a gift when the filming wrapped. She had it still.

Pip wondered where Alain was now. They'd both been in *Pageant Spectacular* in 1982, with Alain as the Silver Knight and Pip as Teacup Beloved, but to her disappointment they'd had no scenes together. His segment had been wrapped the day before she arrived on set, and he'd left the set immediately.

Next time, she'd promised herself. One day. But there hadn't been a next time, or a one day. She'd gone on working steadily into the 2000s but as far as she knew, he hadn't been in anything for years... How old would he be? Maybe in his early seventies. And Varian. Dear, gentle, smooth-gaited Varian would have gone where good horses went a long time ago.

I hope he's grazing in a glory field. Maybe Little Mum will give him an apple. A pippin so he can remember me.

Pip's thoughts faded as she drifted off into sleep.

She dreamed cosily until someone trod on her leg.

CHAPTER TEN. REMEMBERING BANSHEE MARY

Ouch.

The pinching pain, no sooner perceived than gone, woke Pip from her dreams.

Aha…my punishment for being smug.

Glad it had been so mild, she sat up, swag and all.

It was dark in the chartroom by now, but she never had a second's doubt as to where she was.

She heard a gentle chime and a slight intake of breath. She just *knew* whoever made it was trying not to laugh.

"I'm sorry, my maid. Was that your leg?" The voice was a man's, low and light-hearted.

"It still is my leg," Pip responded at a similar volume. "You're lucky I do ballet. Otherwise my muscle tone wouldn't be up to being trodden on."

The treader said, "I didn't see you."

"Looking for someone taller," Pip misquoted.

"Expecting you to be in the cabin, more likely."

"Hmph. Tane, I assume?"

"I am."

Dimly, she perceived movement in front of her, and she put out a tentative hand.

Warm fingers closed around it. "Do you hug, Miss Pearmain?"

"On the whole, never."

She remembered she'd lately made an exception for Jan,

but Jan was family.

"Pity," he said.

"It's not. It saves a great deal of condescension and constriction of my ribs. I don't know which is worse — when people treat me as if I'm made of hollow chocolate or maybe when —" She ran out of comparisons.

He squeezed her hand gently and withdrew. She heard a soft click of fingers and a faint glow bloomed, not from the time-delayed lighting, but from a lantern.

Pip saw it was a dark lantern — one of those with slides that allowed light to be confined to one side. The third crewman set it well back, so it cast its radiance over himself and her while allowing two dark bundles, presumably Jin and Zach, to remain unilluminated.

"So, you are Miss Pippin Pearmain," the crewman said.

"I am." Pip echoed his earlier comment and added waspishly, "Don't loom over me. I don't like it."

"Then you'd better come up on deck so we can talk at proper eyelevel and get to know one another."

"Do I want to know you?"

He smiled. "Most people do."

Pip didn't doubt it. Even if Jin and Zach hadn't mentioned Tane's propensity to be annoying and to proposition random people, she would have spotted his *presence*. As a performer, Pip was well-versed in the awareness of presence. She had it — when she chose. Alain Barfleur had had it in spades. Sully had it, and so, she would bet, did Magda Saxer. Lupin had always had it...Jan didn't.

It wasn't necessarily a good thing to possess. Sully had explained that over a foaming glass of her favourite Fagus Ale one day in a green room. The colour of that beverage had always reminded Pip of peaty mountain creeks. It was beautiful. Pity she didn't like the taste.

After fifty years, she didn't recall Sully's exact words, but the gist of it had been that the right level of presence made one popular and attracted friends and onlookers, while too much could empty the room of anyone who felt overwhelmed and pressured. People without presence could fly under the radar and were nice to be around, but they sometimes had trouble attracting notice when notice was desired.

The best option, in Sully's opinion, was to have it naturally and to learn how to dial it down when necessary.

"Do you do that?" the younger Pip had asked.

"Not bleeding likely." Sully's grin had been ferocious.

How she missed Sully. Even after ten years…

"Are you with me, Miss Pearmain?"

She came back to the present with a snap.

Tane, she judged, had *presence* down to a fine-tuned art and he had just dialled it *up* to get her attention.

"Yes, I'm with you."

"Coming, then?" He gave her a grin that might have been predatory if it hadn't seemed to acknowledge a joke against himself.

Pip bet not many women drifted into memories when Tane-who-couldn't-be-drowned put himself out to be charming.

"I shall," she decided aloud. "However, I *will* not be drawn into gratuitous hugging. Is that understood?"

"Perfectly." He held out a hand. The lamplight made his skin seem faintly gold.

Pip balanced the idea of squirming out of the swag un-aided, which she was perfectly able to do, and allowing him to *help the older lady*.

She took his offered hand. "No yanking. No hauling. Just a bit of moral support for my trodden-on leg."

"I can do that. On the other hand, I could scoop you up, swag and all, and sweep you up the companionway without breaking a sweat."

"You could so," Pip said cordially. She watched the gleam rise in his eyes and added, "And I could squeal like a stuck pig if you tried it. I assure you I have an extremely penetrating squeal. It would wake Jin and Zach and half the fish from here to Christendom. Probably bring the Antarctic whales to check out the danger."

"I know," he said.

"Oh?"

"I heard you employ it when you played Banshee Mary in *Cassidy's Curse*."

Pip felt her eyes bug. She'd forgotten all about *Cassidy's Curse,* and she would have thought everyone else had, too. It had been a six-part children's serial made in the very early 1980s, and as far as she knew, it had never been repeated. That was rather a pity, since she had been proud of the eldritch squeal she and Sully had perfected. Sully said it was *whistle register.* Pip wondered if she could still do it.

She didn't ask where Tane had seen the show. If he'd watched its original airing and remembered her in the role, he must be quite a lot older than he looked.

Maybe someone had taped it.

She used his strong grip to lever herself upright, wiggling free of the cocoon.

"Come on." He tugged at her hand and escorted her to the companionway, swinging the lantern in his spare hand. "Up you go."

Pip said, "You first," determinedly, because she couldn't remember if she'd left her knickers on or not. She suspected she was well beyond the age to have her bottom pinched by even a promiscuous lecher, but she had no desire to find out. If he did anything like that she would be dutybound to squeal, and that would lead to a kerfuffle.

One aborted call to triple zero is enough.

On the other hand, it would be interesting to know if our patented banshee shrill is still available...to stir up whales and chasten would-be lechers.

Chapter Eleven. Fresh Figs

Tane darted up the companionway and onto the deck. Over by the wheelhouse, Pip saw he—or someone—had laid out a mattress and large pillows. A tea-tray rested beside it, and a bowl of something or other sat to one side.

Cosy.

"Make yourself comfortable," he said, gesturing at the nest of pillows.

Pip did so cautiously.

Tane settled across from her, stretching out his legs. He wasn't wearing shoes. Neither was she. Men's feet were usually unattractive. His weren't.

She was glad her toes remained reasonably nice.

She noted he was still bare-chested, and the thing he was wearing looked a bit like an Egyptian kilt. It sparkled and clinked as he moved. He also wore a short silver earring, a chain of silver rings and discs around his neck, and a braided silver ring on his wedding finger.

He should have looked like a desperate drag queen.

"Is that an attempt at chainmail?" she asked, indicating the garment.

"It's my pisky kilt." He patted it affectionately as if it was a favourite pet.

Pip had never heard of one of those, but there was no point asking for clarification, because she could see it. It swung from his hips like the old friend it probably was. It was shaped like a kilt, but it wasn't tartan.

It's not a costume or anything designed to impress. That's just what he wears.

Why not? Men wore skirts in lots of cultures—just not in hers. And she'd always fancied Scotsmen with kilts and pipes and those funny white spats on their shoes.

She looked into his face. One advantage of being over sixty-six was the ability to look at a handsome man without anyone caring or taking it the wrong way. Tane was worth looking at. He had mischievous hazel eyes, ruffled dark blond hair, and his skin really *did* seem faintly gold. He looked a few years older than Zach, who was probably in his early thirties. *Could be forty.* Must be more than that if he remembered her as Banshee Mary.

"You like my silver." He sounded gratified.

She nodded.

"I saw you were admiring it."

"I am. You're a jeweller, so Zach said. Did you make all that regalia yourself?" She'd almost said *bling*, but she had remembered in time the way she'd felt when the jeweller had referred to her heaven and earth ring as *gimcrack*.

"Almost all. I made *these* —" He indicated a row of slightly misshapen charms at the top of the kilt, " —when I was a tiddler. Dad said I had silver in my blood as well as water, and I wanted to prove it. He made the earring for me as soon as I could toddle. He wouldn't let me wear it until I was grown. He said every man should have something lovely to wait for." He reached into the bowl and picked out a plump piece of fruit. "Fresh figs. Want some?"

Pip leaned over and selected one. She noted it was smooth and slightly warm, and far bigger than any self-respecting fig should be.

"Pisky Waters," he said.

"What?"

"That's what I call my design company. Pisky Waters. I specialise in water designs—my logo is three horizontal lines to represent waves. I do commissions for other things, and I make one-off charms. I made a cat charm for Jin, with emerald and sapphire chips for the eyes and rose quartz on the paw pads. I'm not sure she appreciated it."

Pip skirted that idea. Why would Jin not have liked such a thoughtful gift? Maybe because it came with strings attached. But no—she'd said she was safe from Tane's strings.

She said abruptly, "I have a ring I want resized."

"Is it silver? I can work gold and copper, but I'm more attuned to silver."

"I'm pretty sure it's silver...though I don't know how solid. It's quite old, and it has a tiny symbol inside the band. I've had it for nearly sixty years. It's set with a tektite." She told him about it.

"You're not wearing it."

"I need it made smaller...but I don't want it spoiled. I'd rather leave it as it is than have it spoiled."

"I won't spoil it, maid. I've never spoiled anything in my life."

She believed him.

She also saw why Zach seemed ambivalent in his opinion and why Jin and he might brangle. Zach was a nice-looking young man, with a friendly and open face and an athletic figure, but Tane was in her old co-star Alain's league.

"I can look at it for you now," he said, selecting another fig.

Pip got up and took the lantern. She crept down to the chartroom and located her messenger bag. Rather than feel around for the ring in the shadows, she carried the whole bag back on deck.

She saw Tane had poured tea, and for once she decided to drink the Indian brew since she could hardly expect him to go clinking around down in the galley in search of camomile.

Though he must have been down there already to make this lot. Obviously before he trod on me in the chart room.

She dug the ring out of its pouch and dropped it into Tane's waiting palm.

He turned it in his fingers, examining it in the lantern light.

To distract herself—although Zach had assured her Tane wouldn't say anything patronising—she belatedly bit into her fig.

Often, over-sized fruit tasted bland, but that fig was delicious.

Pip held back a moan of delight as the honey-sweet flesh almost dissolved in her mouth.

She's always loved strawberries, but figs like this were her newest favourite fruit.

"Where did you get these?" she asked, indicating the bowl and reaching greedily for another one.

"Kris grows them at the B and B."

Maybe he saw she didn't understand because he added, "Kris is Jin's dad. Calypso, Jin's mum, loves figs. Kris will do anything for Calypso, so he keeps planting fig trees. Even Calypso can't keep up with the fruit-fall, so she gives them to people she likes."

"She likes you?" Pip infused just the right amount of doubt into her query.

"I like her, too," he said, as if that was an answer.

He smiled, waiting until she had finished consuming her fig. Then he held out her ring. "Try it now."

What?

Pip took the ring and slipped it onto her ring finger. To her astonishment, it glided on without fuss and nestled there as if it was custom-made. The tektite stayed right side up.

"How—"

She looked down at it with more attention. The tektite gleamed with its dark secrets and the tooled band retained its patterning. What *had* changed was the size, and the addition of a silver cuff incised with three wavy lines that now lapped the edges and embraced the tektite like a lover.

Tane said, "That's a sweet piece, my maid, full of love and secrets. It's tough enough to stand up to whatever you throw at it."

"How did you do that?"

He shrugged. "Silver in my blood. I resized it to fit your finger. It was easy because it's *you*. I took your hand, remember? How does it feel?"

"At home," Pip said. She turned her hand from side to side, absorbing her delight. "What do I owe you?"

Tane laughed. "I propose a hug."

Pip tossed caution into the wind. "Cheap at twice the price." She got up and struck a theatrical pose. "Come and get it—"

Tane got up in one fluid motion and held out his arms.

Pip went into them and snuggled up. "You smell like my old friend Alain," she said, resting her cheek against his warm chest.

"Oh?"

"Not really. No. Not at all. He smelled of toast. You're more..."

"Bread and apricots, so Jillian says."

"Is that Jillian Jules?" Pip remembered the name from Jin and Zach's banter.

"My love, twice over."

"And how does your love twice over feel about your penchant for hugging stray women?"

He laughed, giving her a gentle squeeze. "Oh, Jill loves hugs. So do our children, and Jill's maid, Sam. They understand hugs are the best currency among friends as well as lovers." He bent and dropped a kiss on her head. "Why not come and meet them!"

"What—now?"

He let go of her and caught her hand. "Yes! Come on... we can all go skinny dipping, and you can dance with the children while Jill and I—" He broke off. "Do come? It will be fun!"

Pip tossed the rest of her cautions to the wind, but before she agreed to his proposition, she said, determinedly, "I'll come to meet your family, but you'll have to let Zach and Jin know beforehand. I don't want them thinking I've gone overboard and come to harm."

Tane said, "Do you really want to wake them?"

"They'll be awake in the morning. Or earlier. Someone must be steering the yacht."

"Would you believe a magic pilot?"

"I would not."

"Automatic pilot?"

"Possibly."

"Do you have some paper? I can write them a note, so they won't be troubled."

Pip disengaged from his hand. She took out her bucket list and carefully removed a page from the back of the feint-lined pad. She handed it to Tane along with the pen.

He scribbled something on the page and stuck the note into the bowl of figs with a fat specimen on top to hold it in place. "Want to read what I wrote?"

"What *did* you write?"

"I said Miss Pearmain has agreed to come and meet my family. I will bring her back to *Tulpenmanie* in time to go back to meet Jamie for her scheduled return home. Does that suffice?"

"That sounds fair enough," she said cautiously.

"Leave your bag next to the figs," he said. "It will be safe. Zach is an honest man and Jin is not the kind of maid to go rifling through another maid's belongings."

Pip left the bag. "I'd better get dressed and drink my tea if I'm coming in the boat with you."

"What boat?" Tane tugged her towards him and scooped her up in his arms. "Ready to go, Miss Pearmain?"

"Yes, but... Wha—" Pip never got the rest of the word out,

let alone the sentence.

Tane jumped up onto the rail and sprang out into the ocean.

AUTHOR'S NOTE

If you've read Lark Westerly's other books, some of the characters in this story might be familiar.

Pippin Pearmain, the cats, and the Pearmain-Laurel-de Leon family all appeared in *Book 1 of* Performing Pippin Pearmain. Prior to that, Pip appeared as a single mention in *Being Tamzin 7.*

Angie Blake's family appeared in retrospect throughout the *Being Tamzin* series.

Zach and Jisinia and the yacht *Tulpenmanie* are all from *Man Overboard.*

Magda Quest Saxer is from the *Pixie Grip* series and *Being Tamzin.*

Oh, you want to know about the bucket that inspired Pip's story?

Read all about it at

http:// performingpippinpearmain.weebly.com/about-the-bucket.html

About the Author

Lark Westerly loves writing series where characters weave in and out of one another's stories.

She also loves playing with ideas and notions and researching odd information.

Lark lives in the island state of Tasmania, where she walks dogs, invents recipes, and goes around in clothes with that lived-in look. She rarely finds a matching pair of socks.

Unlike Pippin Pearmain, Lark is not tiny, not an only child, not single and not an on-screen performer. She never learned ballet and she can't speak Cat-Morse. She doesn't even have a bucket list. Nevertheless, Pippin Pearmain and Lark Westerly are sisters under the skin.

www.ingramcontent.com/pod-product-compliance
Lightning Source LLC
Chambersburg PA
CBHW060637130626
46555CB00002B/845